CH00778609

Giants Round the Corner

and

Other Stories

by
ENID BLYTON

Illustrated by
Lynne Willey

AWARD PUBLICATIONS LIMITED

For further information on Enid Blyton please contact
www.blyton.com

ISBN 1-84135-020-6

This compilation text copyright © 2000 The Enid Blyton Company
Illustrations copyright © 2000 Award Publications Limited

Enid Blyton's signature is a trademark of
The Enid Blyton Company

This edition entitled *Giants Round the Corner and Other Stories*
published by permission of The Enid Blyton Company

This edition first published 2000

Published by Award Publications Limited,
27 Longford Street, London NW1 3DZ

Printed in Singapore

CONTENTS

Giants Round the Corner

Tom and Leonard were the two most annoying boys in the whole school. The girls were afraid of them and the boys disliked them.

They were always playing silly tricks on the girls, bringing mice to school to scare them, and hiding round corners to jump out at them. They fought the boys, because both Tom and Leonard were big and strong, and liked using their fists.

"They're a perfect nuisance!" said Jack, who was getting tired of hearing his little sister complain of being jumped out on, on her way to school. "We shall have to do something about them."

But what? Tom and Lennie were always together, and they were a horrid pair to tackle. They didn't seem to care for anything or anyone. What was to be done?

And then Jessie thought of something. "Can't we give them such a fright that they'll be afraid to do things to us?" she said. "My mother says that bullies are always cowards at heart – so we might be able to scare them."

"Yes. Then we could laugh at them and point our fingers at them, and jeer just as they do to us," said Harry. "It would teach them a lesson. But how are we going to frighten them? Are they frightened of anything? I don't think so."

There was a silence. "Wouldn't they even be afraid of giants?" said a little girl.

Everyone laughed. "Well," said Jack, "I daresay they would be, if we could produce any. But we can't. I don't believe there are any giants nowadays."

"I can make myself into a giant," said the little girl, unexpectedly. Everyone stared at her in surprise.

"What do you mean?" said Harry.

"Well – I'll show you," said Katie, and

she got up. "I only l
won't be long. I'll ma

She hurried off. In
the children heard a
noise, and round t
giantess!

They all leaped to their
Then they laughed. Katie was walking
stilts, very cleverly indeed. She had put
on a very long skirt, so that the stilts
were mostly hidden.

Katie! Can you walk on stilts? ver told us!" cried the children.

ve got them, and so have my two brothers and my sister," said Katie. We can all walk on them very well indeed. And what I'm wondering is, shall I get them to come with me one evening when it's getting dark and hide round a corner, waiting on our tall stilts, and give Tom and Leonard a really terrible fright? Surely they will think we are giants!"

"Oh, yes – it's a wonderful idea!" cried Harry, and everyone agreed. So they began to work out a plan. Katie's two big brothers and her sister, and Katie too, would wrap sheets round themselves to make their legs look very, very long, and then they would wait round a dark corner on their stilts for Tom and Leonard to come.

"You know where Tom and Lennie always wait to jump out at me and Pam?" said Janet. "I know what we'll do. We'll come walking down, so that they'll think just us two girls are coming – and then we'll pop round the corner and Katie

and the others on stilts can take our place. What a terrible shock for Tom and Lennie!"

"Serve them right," said Jack. "It will give them the sort of shock they are always giving other people. It will be a real lesson to them. How I shall laugh. I shall hide myself somewhere to watch."

"My house is just opposite that corner," said Kenneth. "You can all come and watch from the window – except those who are in the performance!"

Well, two evenings later, when it was just beginning to get dark, Tom and Lennie were watching round a corner for Pam and Janet to come along. The little girls always went to a Brownies' meeting that night, and the boys knew it. Tom peeped round and saw the little girls coming.

"They're coming!" he said to Lennie. "What a fright we'll give them!"

But Janet and Pam had slipped aside into the hedge, and out of the hedge had come four enormously tall figures! They stalked down to the corner – and out at them jumped Tom and Lennie!

What a fright the two boys got!

"Who are these two bad boys?" said one of Katie's brothers, in a deep, hollow voice. "Let's eat them."

"I could do with a meal," said another brother in an even deeper voice. "Giants want good meals!"

Tom and Lennie gave shrieks of horror and fled down the road. "No no! Don't eat us! No, no!"

The giants went after them, tap-tapping on the pavement, almost collapsing with laughter. As for the children watching from Kenneth's window, they rolled about with glee. How wonderful the giants had looked

in the twilight! How fast Tom and Lennie had run away!

Next day Tom and Lennie seemed very quiet indeed. They didn't tease anyone, or do any bullying at all.

"What's the matter?" said Harry to them. "Have you had a fright? You didn't see the giants, did you?"

"Giants! Yes – we did see some last night," said Tom, growing pale. "What do you know about them?"

"Oh, nothing much – but we know they were after bad boys – boys who bully and tease," said Harry.

"Katie knows them quite well," said Janet. "I shouldn't be surprised if she told them to lie in wait for you."

"I did," said Katie, with a squeal of laughter. "And they said they had a lovely time frightening you. But they couldn't catch you to eat you."

"Do they – do they really eat boys then?" asked Lennie, scared.

"Why not let them catch you next time, and then you'll see if you're eaten or not," said Katie. "You see, they are only after horrid children, so it's no good us waiting about for them. They're after you two boys."

Well, that was quite enough for Tom and Lennie. They turned over a new leaf, and were quite different. Jessie's mother had been quite right when she said that bullies are always cowards at heart – their fright taught them a lesson, and they never scared or bullied anyone again.

I would have loved to see those "giants", wouldn't you? Wasn't it a good idea of Katie's?

13

Stamp-About's Spell

One day Mr Stamp-About went through Dimity Wood in a great rage. He stamped as he went, and muttered to himself, and he even shook his fist in the air.

"I'll pay old Snorty out for not giving me what he owes me! How am I to pay my bills if he doesn't pay his! How dare he say that the apples I sold him were bad, and not worth a penny? How dare he not pay me for them!"

The rabbits fled away from his stamping feet, and the squirrels bounded up into the trees. The robin followed him, flying from tree to tree in wonder. *Now* what was the matter with noisy old Stamp-About?

Stamp-About didn't notice that he had taken the wrong path in the wood. He went on and on, and then suddenly found that the path was getting very narrow. He stopped and looked round.

"I've taken the wrong path! All because of Snorty! I am so angry with him that I don't even see the way I am walking!"

He stood there a few moments, wondering what to do.

"Perhaps there's someone nearby who will hear me if I shout, and tell me the right path," he thought. So he gave a loud shout: "Ho there! I want help!"

Nobody answered at all, and the birds all flew away in fright, for Stamp-About had such a tremendous voice! He yelled again.

"I said, 'Ho there! I want help!'"

And this time a voice called back to him – a very cross voice indeed.

"Will you be quiet? You're spoiling my spell!"

Stamp-About couldn't believe his ears. Spoiling someone's spell? Whose? And if the someone was near enough to shout back, why didn't he come to Stamp-About's help? "Rude fellow!" thought Stamp-About, angrily. "I'll go and tell him what I think of him!"

So he pushed his way fiercely through the bushes, and came upon a little clearing, set neatly round with spotted red toadstools in a ring. In the middle sat a little fellow in a long black cloak that shimmered like moonlight. He had two long feelers on his forehead, the same shape as a butterfly's.

In front of him a small fire burned, and on it was a bowl of clear glass which,

strangely enough, seemed not to mind the flames at all.

"Why didn't you come to my help?" stormed Stamp-About.

"For goodness sake go away," said the little fellow, turning round. "Yelling like that in my spell time! I never heard of such a thing. Go and buy yourself a few manners!"

Stamp-About almost exploded with temper. "How dare you!" he cried. "Who are you, you – you miserable, uncivil little fellow?"

"I'm Weeny, the little wizard," said the small man. "And I get my living by making spells at this time each day and selling them. And then you come blustering along and spoil them all. Just when I was making gold, too! Pah!"

"*Gold?*" said Stamp-About, in quite a different voice. "Good gracious – can you make gold?"

"Not exactly," said the little wizard. "But my spells can. I've only to pop the right things into my little glass bowl here, and spell each one as they dissolve – and at the end, what do I find? A handful of gold at the bottom of my bowl!"

"Really?" said Stamp-About, wishing he hadn't been rude. "Er – I'm sorry I disturbed you. Pray start all over again! But why do you have to spell each word – why can't you just say it?"

"Don't be silly," said the little wizard. "A spell is a spell because it's spelled, isn't it? You can't make a spell unless you spell it, can you?"

"I don't know," said Stamp-About, and

18

came into the toadstool ring, treading on one as he did so.

"Get out!" said the wizard, pointing a long thin finger at him. "Treading on my magic toadstool! Get out! I'll turn you into a worm and call down that robin over there if you're not careful!"

Stamp-About hurriedly stepped out of the ring of toadstools, being very careful not to break one again.

"Now go away, and let me start my gold-spell all over again," commanded the fierce little fellow. Stamp-About tiptoed away and hid behind a tree. All right – let the wizard order him about all he liked – he would hide and watch the spell and then he would make it too, when he got home! Aha – gold for the making – what a wonderful thing!

He peeped from behind a tree and watched. The wizard took no more notice of him. He had a pile of things to put

into the glass bowl – but first he poured into it some water from a little jug.

Then he took up a buttercup and shredded its golden petals one by one into the bowl, muttering as he did so. Stamp-About strained his ears, but he couldn't catch what was being said, until he heard the wizard say "C-U-P."

"Of course – he's only spelling the name of the flower," thought Stamp-About. "Now – what's he putting in this time? Oh – one of the red toadstools. And now he's spelling that. Ho – what an easy spell to make!"

He watched carefully. The little wizard took another buttercup and spelled out its name – then he took a twig of hawthorn blossom and shook the white petals into the bowl, and then another buttercup.

"He's spelling everything," thought Stamp-About. "Well, who would have thought that spelling had anything to do with the making of spells! This is going to be very useful to me! Now what's he taking?"

The wizard had now picked up the empty shell of a robin's egg, and had crushed it up and dropped it into the bubbling water, which was now changing to all colours. He muttered as he spelled the name, and then threw in yet another shower of buttercup petals.

Then he danced lightly round the bowl three times and stopped. To Stamp-About's astonishment all the water in the bowl rose up as a cloud of steam – and there, left at the bottom, was a gleaming handful of gold!

"Look at that!" whispered Stamp-About to himself in glee, as he watched the wizard put the gold into a wallet.

"Now I know exactly how to make the spell. I'll go home and do it."

The little wizard took up the bowl, put it into a small bag, and then he stamped out the fire. He disappeared like a shadow through the trees.

"I'll follow him," thought Stamp-About. "He must know the way out of this wood."

So he followed carefully, and soon came to a path he knew. He went one way and the little wizard went the other. Stamp-About was so excited that he went home smiling all over his face – much to the surprise of Snorty, who was leaning over his gate as Stamp-About passed.

"Ho! You're in a better temper now, are you?" called Snorty. "Well, perhaps now you'll admit that those apples of yours were bad – and that I don't owe you for them after all!"

"I don't need a penny from you, Snorty, not a penny!" said Stamp-About. "I shall soon be rich. I shall pay all the bills I haven't paid – and you'll come borrowing from me, you see if you don't!"

Well, this was very astonishing news to Snorty, who soon spread it about that Stamp-About was going to be rich. "How?" said his friends. "What's he going to do? Let's go round and ask him."

When they came to Stamp-About's house he was out in his garden. He had made a small fire in the middle of the lawn, and on it he had placed a little glass bowl – the one in which his goldfish once used to swim.

"Look at that!" said Snorty in amazement. "What's he doing? See – he's got a pile of strange things beside him – buttercups – a red toadstool – and what's that – the shell of an egg? And look, there's a spray of hawthorn blossom too, off the may hedge."

Stamp-About saw everyone watching and was very pleased to show off. He did exactly as he had seen the little wizard do – first he threw in the buttercup petals, shredding them off the flower head one by one. As he did so, he spelled the name out loud in a high chanting voice:

"B-U-T-E-R-C-U-P!"

24

Then he took up the red toadstool and put that into the bowl of water too. Again he chanted out loud, spelling the name clearly:

"R-E-D-T-O-D-E-S-T-O-O-L!"

Then he shredded buttercup petals again and spelled the name as before, and then took the hawthorn blossom.

"H-O-R-T-H-O-R-N!"

And in went the white may petals as he shook the twig over the bowl! Aha – the water was changing to all kinds of colours now. Soon the handful of gold would be there!

In went more buttercup petals and the name was spelled: "B-U-T-E-R-C-U-P!" Then he picked up the broken shell of a robin's egg.

As he crumpled up the shell and it fell into the water Stamp-About spelled out the name in a loud voice:

"R-O-B-B-I-N-S-E-G-G!"

And last of all another shower of golden buttercup petals went into the bubbling water. Eagerly Stamp-About leaned over it. Now for the gold! First the water would disappear in a cloud of steam – and then he would see the handful of gold at the bottom. But wait – first he must dance three times round the bowl.

Everyone crept forward to see what was about to happen. A cloud of steam shot high into the air and the water in the bowl disappeared. Then the bowl

itself exploded with such a bang that everyone fell over backwards. Stamp-About sat down very suddenly indeed, scared almost out of his wits.

Then he looked eagerly at the fire – where was the gold? Had it been scattered about all round it?

No – there wasn't a single piece of gold.

The fire had gone out when the bowl exploded and now only one thing lay there – a large book!

"What's happened?" shouted Stamp-About in a rage. "The spell's gone wrong! It should have made gold, not a stupid book. What book is it?"

He picked it up and opened it – then he looked up in astonishment and everyone crowded round to see what it was.

"It's a dictionary!" said Snorty and gave a huge guffaw. "Ha-ha, ho-ho – I'm not surprised."

"But – why did the spell go wrong?" cried Stamp-About, and dashed the book to the ground. "I don't want a dictionary!"

"Yes, you do!" chuckled Snorty. "The spell went wrong because your spelling went wrong! Spells have to be spelled correctly! That's why all you've got is a dictionary – to help you to spell. Oh, ho-ho-ho-ho – what a joke! Can you spell rotten apples, Stamp-About? Oh, what a comical thing! He tried to make a spell – but he couldn't even spell!"

It was quite true. The spell wouldn't work unless everything was spelled out correctly, and Stamp-About had conjured up something he needed as much as gold – a dictionary. Poor old Stamp-About – he hasn't paid his bills yet!

Come On,
Wags!

"I'm going to take Wags for a walk, Mum!" called Pat. "I'll be back in good time for tea. Come on, Wags. It's a lovely windy day, just right for a walk!"

Wags ran up, his tail wagging so fast that Pat could hardly see it! "I never knew a dog with such a waggy tail as you!" he said. "No wonder we called you Wags. And when you've got your mouth open and your tongue out, you look exactly as if you're smiling."

Wags loved a walk. He didn't mind where he went, so long as he was with Pat. He often wondered why the boy didn't bend down and sniff here and there, to smell all the wonderful smells in the woods, or along the lanes. What a lot Pat was missing!

"You know, Wags, you need a new collar," said Pat. "Yours is dreadfully old, and it's really too small for you now. But I simply can't seem to save up enough money to get you a new one. You see, it's always someone's birthday, or else it's Christmas, or else it's holidays by the sea. As soon as I've enough in my money-box to buy you a collar, I have to spend the money on something else!"

"Wuff, wuff," said Wags, wagging his tail happily, and smiling up at Pat. What did he care about a new collar? He wasn't a fussy dog at all!

They went through the woods, where all the trees were swaying about in the wind, and came back by the park. Pat stopped at the gates and looked into the park in surprise.

"There must be something on," he said. "Look at the crowd of people there, Wags. And there are some tents. Shall we go and see what's happening?"

"Wuff," answered Wags at once, and scampered into the park. They soon found out what the show was.

"It's a flower show," said Pat, "and a vegetable show, too. Well, that's not very interesting to you and me, Wags. But what's in this tent here? I can hear a lot of barking!"

Pat stopped outside the tent and looked at a poster there. "Dog show!" he said. "Fancy that! No wonder there's so much barking! Well, I can't put you on show, Wags, old thing – you're just a very, very ordinary dog, even though you are the nicest dog in the world. Come along – we'll go home."

Wags was disappointed. He would have

loved to peep into the dog tent, and say how-do-you-do to the dogs there. He was sure he could hear the bark of Rufus the dog next door. Perhaps Rufus would win a prize; yes, he was sure to. He was the most beautiful silky spaniel that Wags had ever seen, and very, very haughty towards common little dogs like Wags.

But Pat was already some way away, and Wags scampered after him. The wind blew his ears back, and ruffled his hairy coat. Wuff! Wags liked the wind. It made him feel quite mad, and he leaped about joyfully.

He didn't see a man get up from a nearby seat, holding on to his hat. He rushed right into him, got between the man's legs, and bowled him over. *Bump!* Down the man went, most surprised. He let go of his hat, and the wind pounced down and took it from his head. *Whooosh!* Away it went, bowling along the path like a live thing, over and over and over!

"Wuff!" Wags gave the man a hurried lick to show he was sorry for knocking him over, and then tore after the hat. Each time he thought he had it, the wind blew a little harder, and Wags simply could not get hold of it.

Away it went, bowling along – down the path, over the grass, across another path – and right into the tent where the dog show was being held! And after it went Wags, of course, racing through the tent opening at top speed. The hat came to rest in the middle of the dog-ring, and Wags pounced on it joyfully.

He took it into his mouth and then had a look round. Good gracious! What a lot of dogs were in the ring! Big dogs, and little ones, fat ones and thin ones, common ones and shining, beautiful ones. Wags sat down in the very middle, the hat still in his mouth. He meant to watch what happened.

Pat appeared in the tent to look for Wags. He was most astonished to see him sitting down right in the middle of the ring, hat in mouth.

"Wags!" he called, but Wags couldn't hear him, there was so much barking.

"Who owns this dog?" shouted a voice. "Will the owner please come to him?"

Pat stepped into the ring, and went up to Wags. "Please stay there," said the man. "We are about to judge the dogs."

"But – but my dog isn't . . ." began Pat, and stopped when he saw that nobody was listening to him. "Here, Wags – we'd better go," he said. But Wags was not going. This was fun.

Two judges were now going to each dog. The dogs were held by their owners, all children. At first Pat couldn't make out how they were being judged – and then he laughed.

"Why – they're judging their tails!" he said. "Fancy that! Well, I'm afraid you haven't a beautiful tail, Wags, or you might have gone in for such a funny competition!"

But the tails were not being judged for their beauty, or hairiness, or length. They were being judged for their wags! Well, well, well!

"Let me see your dog wag its tail," said one of the judges to a small girl. She bent down and patted her dog. "Good dog," she said, "good dog!" And, of course, the

dog wagged its tail in pleasure. Then the next dog had to wag its tail, too, but it was frightened, and put it between its legs! The judges turned to Pat. "What about your dog?" one said. "Let us see what kind of a wag his tail has."

Pat stared at the judges in surprise. "He's got a very waggy tail," he said, patting Wags. "Why, we even had to call him Wags! Wags, show what your tail can do! Good dog, then, good dog, best dog in the world!"

Wags was so very pleased at being called the best dog in the world in front of so many people that he went nearly mad with delight. He stood there, wagging his tail so fast that it made quite a wind round the judges' legs!

Then he sat down, and thumped his tail on the ground. *Thump, thump, THUMP! Thump, thump, THUMP!* Everyone began to laugh, because it looked as if Wags was showing off his wagginess in every way he could!

"A very fine wag indeed," said one of the judges, laughing. "Wait here, boy. So far your dog has the waggiest tail of all."

Would you believe it, Wags won the prize! Pat stared in astonishment as the judges came back to Wags and patted him. They handed Pat an envelope.

"Your dog has the most wag in his tail of all the dogs here," said one. "He wins the prize. Well done!"

"But – but I didn't really put him in the show," said Pat. "It was quite an accident. He didn't . . ."

"Well, accident or not, he's won the prize," said the judge, laughing. "Take him away now. We're judging cats next

and we want all the dogs well away from here."

Pat hurried Wags away. At the tent door stood the man whose hat had been blown off. He was looking anxiously round to see if it was anywhere about. Wags had picked it up again and was trotting along with it, looking about for the owner. He dropped it at the man's feet and then rolled over on his back, all four paws in the air.

"That's his way of saying he's sorry he bumped into you and knocked you over, sir," said Pat, hoping that the man wasn't going to be angry.

"Oh – well, I'll forgive him then," said the man, brushing the dust from his hat. "I see he's won a prize. What is he good at, besides knocking people over?"

"He's got the best wag in his tail – better than any other dog's," said Pat, proudly. "But if he hadn't knocked you over and then run into the tent to get your hat back, he'd never have been in the show at all."

"Well, I'm glad I've been of some use to you," said the man, putting on his hat. "Congratulations, dog, on being such a fine tail-wagger!"

Pat went off with Wags. He stopped under a tree to open the envelope. Good gracious! There was ten pounds in it!

"Wags! Your tail has won you ten pounds," he said. "Enough to buy you a new collar – and to get Mum and you and me some ice cream for tea. Come on – we'll go and spend it!"

So away they went, Wags bounding along and wagging his tail faster than ever. What an afternoon! He was sorry Pat hadn't a tail to wag, too!

The Bold
Bad Boys!

Derek and Tom loved to go down and play beside the river. They liked watching the boats go by, and when a launch floated along in midstream, making quite big waves break against the banks, they shouted with joy.

"Dad, can't we have a boat of our own?" begged Derek. "Lots of the boys we know have. Why can't we?"

"For a very good reason," said their father. "You can't swim yet! I tried to teach you last summer, but you both cried because the water was cold, and Tom yelled when I held him up and tried to make him do the arm-strokes."

The boys looked ashamed. "If you'd let us have a boat, we promise we'll learn to swim this summer," said Derek.

41

"Oh, no!" said Father. "*I'll* promise you a boat *when* you have learned to swim. That's the right way to put it."

The boys went off, rather sulky. "Lots of people who can't swim have boats," said Tom. "How can we have adventures, and go rowing off to find them, if we haven't got a boat. Dad's mean."

"Never mind," said Derek. "We'll have a good time paddling. We'll call ourselves the Bold Bad Boys and we'll look for adventures every single day. We'll be pirates and smugglers, and we'll be very bold and daring."

So they were. They became a great nuisance to the moorhens by the river, and the big swans hissed at them as they sailed grandly by. But when the cows came down to stand in the shallow part of the river, the bold bad boys ran away. They were rather afraid of cows!

Now, one day, when the two boys were sitting by the water, splashing it with their feet, they saw something coming down the river. It wasn't a boat. It wasn't a bird. What could it be?

"It's a barrel! An empty barrel, floating along all by itself!" cried Derek. "If only we could get it on to the bank, Tom. We could play smugglers properly if we had a barrel of our own! We could even hide in it."

They watched the barrel. It came bobbing along – and floated to where a low branch stretched out from the bank over the water. There it caught and stopped.

"Look, look!" cried Derek. "It's caught on that branch. Oh, Tom, let's be really bold and crawl out on the branch and get the barrel. I think the water is shallow there, and maybe we could get on the barrel and push it over to the bank."

So, feeling very bold and daring, the two boys crawled along the branch to the barrel. Derek leaned down and caught hold of it.

"Tom, can you get on to the barrel while I hold it?" he said. "Quick, in case I have to let go. That's right. Oh good, you're riding the barrel! Will it take me too, do you think?"

Tom had dropped neatly on to the barrel, and was now riding astride it, grinning happily. Derek dropped down beside him.

Now they were both on the barrel. "Work hard with your feet and we'll get it to the bank," said Derek. But alas, as soon as they left the tree branch, the barrel, instead of going towards the bank, got caught by the midstream current and swung out into deep water. Then it began floating merrily down the river with the two boys riding it!

Tom screamed. "Derek, Derek! We're out in deep water. We'll drown!"

"Not if we cling to the barrel," said Derek, going rather white.

"Hold on, Tom. Don't let go whatever you do. Oh, gracious, we're going quite fast."

"I feel sick, I feel sick," wailed Tom. "I want to be rescued. Oooooooh!"

Derek was scared, too. He clung to the bobbing barrel and looked round to see if any boats were about. Not one was anywhere to be seen. So on they bobbed and on and on.

Then suddenly a fisherman by the river saw them. "Help, help!" cried Derek. "Save us!"

The fisherman ran to a small boat nearby and got into it. With three or four strong pulls at the oars he was soon alongside the barrel. He pulled the boys into the boat. Tom burst into wails.

"We were nearly drowned. Take me home to Mummy."

The fisherman rowed to the shore. He found out where Tom and Derek lived and took them both back home, wet and scared. Their father came out when he saw them.

"Whatever's the matter?" he said. "Have you fallen in the river?"

"No, oh no!" wailed Tom. "We saw a barrel floating down and we crawled out on a tree branch to it . . ."

"And got on it, meaning to take it to the bank, and it floated away with us," said Derek.

"I rescued them in time," said the fisherman, winking at Father. "Seems to me they're strange boys, not liking an adventure. Most boys are looking out for one every day."

"So are Tom and Derek," said their father. "In fact, I believe they call themselves the Bold Bad Boys, and half the time they're smugglers and pirates. And when a little adventure like this comes along, they yell and howl and can't bear it! Well, well, well!"

"Why didn't they swim to shore?" asked the fisherman, surprised to hear all this.

"I'm sorry to have to tell you – but both boys are too scared to learn to swim," said Father, solemnly. "They want a boat – and yet they can't swim!"

"Well, they had a barrel for a boat, and they didn't seem to like that at all," said the fisherman. "I reckon a boat would be wasted on them."

"Just what I think," said Father. "Well, thanks for rescuing them. Maybe one day they will welcome an adventure when they get one, instead of howling about it."

"Thank you for rescuing us, sir," said Derek, his face very red indeed. He felt so ashamed. To think they were the two bold bad boys, always looking out for an adventure, and now they had behaved like this!

Derek took Tom into the garden into their secret corner. "We're going to learn to swim!" he told Tom fiercely. "Do you hear, Tom? And there's to be no moaning and groaning about it. We're going to make Dad proud of us for a change!"

Well, the last time I saw Derek and

Tom they were in a small, neat boat of their own, rowing out on the river. So I knew they had learned to swim and could really look for exciting adventures. Do you know what they have called their boat? It's called *The Bold Bad Boys*, of course.

The Boy Who
Turned Into an Engine

There was once a boy called Thomas who simply loved playing at engines. He put his hands up before him to make the buffers of an engine, and then raced round the garden, puffing for all he was worth!

You could hear him any day – ch-ch-ch-ch-ch-ch-ch! Mrs Brown next door knew when he was in the garden because she could hear the "ch-ch-ch", and the "oooooo" that Thomas made when he whistled like an engine.

The grocer knew when Thomas ran by each day because he too heard "ch-ch-ch-ch" and "oooooo". Mrs Penny, who liked to snooze in a chair in her front garden, was often woken up with a jump when the little Thomas-engine went rushing by her gate: "ch-ch-ch-ch." He always gave a loud "oooooo" just there because her house was supposed to be a tunnel.

"One day, Thomas," said his mother, "you will certainly turn into an engine! Couldn't you be a car for a change, or an aeroplane?"

"No, Mummy," said Thomas. "I love engines best. I like to pretend to be an engine all the time. Oh, how I wish I was an engine-driver!"

Now one day, when the sun shone out warmly and daffodils nodded everywhere, the wind blew from the south-west. As I daresay you know, Fairyland lies to the south-west, and the wind had blown from there. And that day there was magic in the wind!

It had blown over Witch Humpy's house and she had been making spells that morning in a big pot over her fire. The steam from the pot had mixed with the green smoke that came out of her chimney and the wind had taken it to play with. It blew it here and there before

it – and it so happened that it blew the magic steam and smoke over Thomas as he ran puffing "ch-ch-ch-ch-ch!" by the side of the railway track. "Ooooooo" shouted Thomas, as he went, just like a real train coming in at the station.

"Ooooo-oo!" shouted the wind and puffed the bit of witch-smoke into Thomas's face.

And in that very moment Thomas changed into a real engine! He found himself rushing along a railway track. He was shouting "ch-ch-ch-ch!" very quickly and very loudly indeed. Thomas tried to look down at his feet to see how it was that he was going so quickly.

But he had no feet – only great wheels that tore round and round and round as he went! Thomas was so astonished that he nearly ran off the track!

"I've changed into an engine!" he thought to himself. "A real engine! However did it happen? I wonder how loud I can whistle now."

He whistled – "OOOOOOOOOOOOO". My goodness, it was so loud that Thomas made himself jump. He wobbled a bit on the track and felt quite scared.

"I must be careful," he thought. "It won't do to get off the track. There might be an accident. I wonder if I've got any carriages behind me."

He looked to see – and to his delight he found that he had about twelve carriages in a row, all tearing after him. Just at the back of him was the coal-truck full of coal. In his cab burned a big fire and a driver and stoker stood there, talking. People sat in the carriages and read their papers. The train was going a very long way.

"Ch-ch-ch-ch-ch!" went Thomas in

delight. My, it was fine to be a real train, on a real track, instead of just a pretend one, going down the road. He thundered through stations, and whistled at the top of his voice: "Ooooooooo!"

He ran under long, dark tunnels, and once he was very frightened to see what he thought was a big black animal with red eyes coming towards him in a tunnel – but it was only another train going the opposite way. Thomas laughed and let off steam. It made a great chuffy noise and startled all the cows in a nearby field.

On he thundered, and on. He went over a bridge and looked down into a deep river. He stopped once at a busy station and people jumped in and out of the carriages. Thomas was quite glad of the rest. He stood there, puffing and blowing.

Then he whistled again, "OOOOOO," and set off once more. "Ch-ch-ch-ch-ch!" He raced through the countryside joyfully, and the driver turned to the stoker in surprise.

"My, isn't the engine going well today," he said. "Like a little boy running home from school!"

At last Thomas came to a seaside station. He could go no further, for the blue sea lay in front of him. He stopped and everyone got out. Thomas felt terribly thirsty. The driver ran him to a big tank and let down a hose. Thomas had a long, long drink. How delicious it was!

In a little while it was time for Thomas to start back. He saw the people getting into the carriages. He was longing to go. He puffed impatiently – "ch-ch-ch-ch-ch!" Then he gave a piercing whistle, and made a dog jump almost out of its skin, and a little girl began to cry!

At last Thomas was off once more. He thundered down the track, chuffing out white smoke, and whistling whenever he came to a level-crossing. He shot in and out of the tunnels. He clattered over bridges and shrieked through stations, having a perfectly glorious time!

And then he came to his own station at home. And do you know, as he watched the people getting out of the carriages, he saw his own father! Yes, there he was getting out of the train to go home!

Thomas was so pleased to see him. He shouted loudly, "Daddy! Daddy!" But his voice turned into a loud whistle, and his father didn't hear his name being called.

He walked on towards the station gate.

"Daddy, look at me, I'm a real engine!" shouted Thomas, and he tried to run after his father. He got off the track – he jumped on to the platform – he rushed after his father!

But nobody seemed surprised to see an engine get off the track and on to the platform – because, as soon as he left the track Thomas became himself again! He tore over the platform on two legs, his hands held up as if they were engine buffers, and came up to his father.

"Hello, hello, hello!" said Father, as he heard the "ch-ch-ch-ch!" and the loud "oooooo!" beside him. "Here's the little Thomas-engine again! One of these days, Thomas, you will certainly turn into an engine and go tearing down the track!"

"That's just what I have been doing today!" said Thomas. But Father only laughed. He didn't believe him at all.

So now Thomas is waiting to change into an engine again – and then he is going to jump off the railway track, go puffing down the road and up to the front door of his home. He thinks his parents will believe his tale then.

Wouldn't you love to be there when he comes chuffing up, "ch-ch-ch-ch!" I would. What a surprise it will be to see a real train come up the garden path!

They Said He
Was Too Small

"Clear off!" yelled Dick to Joe. "I've told you before, you're too small to play football with us!"

"I'm only a year younger than you!" yelled back Joe. "And I'm a jolly good player, too!"

"You're not. You're too small to make a good footballer!" shouted Dick. "You're a shrimp. Clear off!"

A boy near Joe gave him a shove. "Go on – do what Dick says. He's the captain. We can't have tiddlers like you playing with us."

"I can't help being small," said Joe, angrily. "I'll grow, won't I? Give me a chance. I've a big uncle who was a famous footballer, and I'm going to be like him. Give me a chance."

But all he got was another shove which sent him flying to the ground. Joe got up and walked off crossly, wishing and wishing that he was as tall as the others.

He went home. His mother was surprised to see him. "I thought you were playing football, Joe," she said. "Aren't the boys playing today?"

"Yes. But they told me to clear off," said Joe, miserably. "I'm too small. Can't I do anything to make myself grow, Mum? I'm a fast runner and a good kicker, and I just don't care how often I get tripped up."

"Cheer up, Joe," said his mother. "I've some news for you. Uncle Jim is visiting Granny today. You know what a great footballer he was until he hurt his back. You go and talk to him about football. He'll tell you plenty of good tales."

Joe sped off, thrilled. Uncle Jim had been such a wonderful footballer, it would be marvellous to see him again and hear his tales. He might give Joe a few tips, too, on playing football.

Uncle Jim was at Granny's. Granny was his mother, and she was delighted to see him. She gave Joe a great welcome, too. "Ah – my two footballers!" she said. "Now, Jim, you just talk to Joe while I get the lunch."

"Why aren't you out playing football this lovely Saturday morning?" asked Uncle Jim. "I wouldn't have wasted a fine day like this when I was your age, if I could have been out on the football ground."

"I feel like that, too," said Joe. "But the boys won't let me join their team. They say I'm a shrimp and a tiddler and much

63

too small. All the same, I'm nearly as old as some of them."

Uncle Jim saw that Joe was very miserable although he tried to smile. "Never mind – we'll find one of my old footballs up in Granny's attic, and have a game to ourselves!" he said. So up he went and rummaged about, and soon came down again with a marvellous football. He made it ready for play and Joe looked on, excited. "What is all this writing on the ball, Uncle?" he asked, running his finger over some faded words.

"Ah – those are the signatures of many famous footballers," said his uncle. "They gave me this football when I had to retire because of my back, and they signed their names on it. I think perhaps I'll give it to you, Joe – I shall never use it in a game again."

Joe could hardly believe his ears. What! Have this magnificent football, with the autographs of famous footballers all over it! Why – goodness me – whatever would the boys say!

"Come on," said Uncle Jim. "We'll have a game and I'll give you a few hints. We'll have fun!"

They did have fun, and when Joe went home at lunch-time his face shone like the sun. He had had a wonderful morning – and now he owned a marvellous football! He would take it out to the field that very afternoon and kick it around.

So he went out that sunny afternoon and was soon kicking it round the field. Tom came up to him. "That's a fine football. Where did you get it?"

"It belonged to my Uncle Jim – the one who was a footballer," said Joe. "And look – it has the autographs of all the famous players written on it. It's really too valuable to play with – but I simply must have a kick around!"

Tom went to find Dick, the captain. "I say," he said, "that shrimp Joe has a simply magnificent football – look at it. It's much better than our old thing. It's got famous footballers' names signed all over it, too."

"Go and ask him to join in our game, and see if he'll let us play with his football," said Dick at once. So off went Tom back to Joe.

"Dick says you can play with us this afternoon – and bring that ball along with you," he said.

"No thanks," said Joe. "I'm not big enough to play with you. You've said so dozens of times. I'll just kick it around by myself."

Soon all the boys were watching Joe as he kicked the wonderful football about. "Come on, Joe!" yelled John. "Come and

play. Let's have a kick at that ball."

"I'm too small to play with you," said Joe. "You keep saying so. You only want me in because I've got this ball. And let me tell you this – my Uncle Jim played football with me this morning, and he gave me some good hints. I bet we'd win our next match if I told them to you."

"You come on and play, Joe," said Dick. "We do want your ball, it's true – but if you play well, we'll want you too. Come on – we're a boy short."

Joe grinned. He had meant to play all the time. He kicked the ball to Dick. "All right," he said. "I'll make a bargain with you. If I play well you'll let me into the team with my ball. But if I've told a fib, and I play badly, well, kick me out – but I'll still lend you my ball. How's that?"

"You're a good littl'un," said Dick, and gave him slap on the back. "Right. It's a bargain!"

Well, you should have seen Joe that afternoon. He ran like a hare. He shot two goals. He took the ball from the other side time after time. He tried out all the

tricks his uncle had shown him. He fell heavily at least six times but he was up and running again at once. And how marvellous that ball was compared with the old one the boys had played with for weeks!

The game was over at last. The boys clustered round Joe, panting. Dick gave him such a slap on the back that the small boy almost fell over.

"You win, Joe! You're in the team. You may be a tiddler, but, my word, you're a good tiddler! We can do with someone like you!"

"You're sure I'm not too small for you?" said Joe, slyly.

"We're sure – so long as you're sure we're not too big for you!" said Dick. "You go along and tell your uncle we like his ball – and we like his nephew even better!"

Well, wasn't that good? Joe's grown up now and he's a wonderful footballer. You've read his name in the paper many a time!

The Greedy
Little Sparrow

Feathers was a greedy little brown sparrow who was always first on the bird-table and last to go. How he loved the crusts, bacon rinds and scraps that Hannah and Frank put out every morning!

He wished he could keep all the other birds away from the table so that he might have even more to eat. But how could he do that?

"I know!" he said at last. "I'll say that the black cat is about. Then the others will be careful and I shall be able to eat all I want to."

So, the next morning, when Hannah and Frank put food on their bird-table, Feathers began to chirrup loudly to the others.

"Chirrup! Chirrup! Be careful! Be careful! Chirrup! The cat's about! Chirrup! She's hiding under a bush; I saw her! Chirrup! She is waiting for us to go on the bird-table and then she will pounce! Chirrup!"

All the birds heard this warning cry and stayed quietly in the bushes and on the gutter. Every one was afraid of the cat. No one wanted to be caught by Sooty, whose sharp claws could strike down even a big bird like Glossy the blackbird.

"I'll fly down to the bird-table and see if Sooty is anywhere about still!" Feathers chirruped shortly. "Keep where you are, everybody! I'll fly down!"

He flew down – and in a second was pecking hard at the breadcrumbs there. "Chirrup!" he called to the others. "Be careful! I think I can see the cat under the lilac bush! I'll tell you when she goes!"

Feathers had another good peck at the food, pretending to keep a watch for the cat every now and again. The other birds watched him hungrily – but no one ventured to fly down. They were dreadfully afraid of Sooty the cat.

Then the starling, who had been sitting on the chimney-top warming his toes, suddenly gave a splutter. "Why! There's Sooty in the next-door garden! She can't be hiding under the lilac bush!"

Sure enough, when the birds looked, there was Sooty lying peacefully in the next garden, asleep in the sun. One by one the birds flew down to the table and were soon enjoying a good meal. But Feathers had taken all the best titbits, you may be sure.

The next day Feathers went on with his trick. As soon as Hannah and Frank had filled the bird-table with scraps, and the birds had flown down to them, Feathers, who was sitting on the gutter, gave a loud chirrup.

"Chirrup! Chirrup! Fly away quickly! I can see a tabby-cat round by that tub! He's watching you all! He's going to pounce! Chirrup!"

With a flutter of wings and squawks of fright all the sparrows, chaffinches, starlings and thrushes flew off the bird-table. Some went to the bushes, some

flew to the roof, and others were so frightened that they flew to the fields. Feathers was pleased. He flew down to the bird-table at once and called to the others.

"I'll keep my eye on that tabby-cat! I can see him from here! I'll tell you when he's gone! Oh, you bad cat, I can see you, yes, I can see you! Chirrup, chirrup!"

"Isn't Feathers brave?" said a little chaffinch with a bright pink chest.

"He's wonderful the way he sees any hiding cat," said a cock-sparrow.

"And it's very plucky of him to wait on the table and tell us when the cat is gone," said a gleaming starling. "That cat might easily pounce on him."

Feathers heard what everyone was saying and he chirruped in delight to himself. He was doing something very mean – and here were the others praising him and thinking him such a fine, brave fellow.

"I'm clever, I am," thought Feathers. "They're all stupid. I'm the only clever one. See how easily I am tricking them! I

keep them all away from the food till I've taken the best."

He pecked away busily, pretending to keep an eye on the cat all the time. Then, when he had eaten all the best scraps, he chirruped to the others, "You can come down to the table safely now, for the cat has gone. I saw him slink away. He's afraid of me!"

The birds flew down and fed. They were very polite to Feathers, for they all thought he was a charming and helpful fellow.

The next day Feathers spied some cake-crumbs in the next-door-but-one-garden. He loved these, for they were sweet. The children had eaten their tea in the garden and had left a great many cake-crumbs about. Feathers was pleased.

"Nobody else seems to have seen them," said Feathers to himself. "That's lucky. I shan't share them with anyone. I'll just fly down and get them."

As he was about to fly down, a small hen-sparrow chirruped to him from the roof, "Feathers! Feathers! Be careful! There is a big Persian cat in the garden! Don't go down for those cake-crumbs!"

"Oho!" said Feathers to himself, with a quick look round. "So there is another sparrow who is playing my trick and pretending there are cats about so that she can get the crumbs herself! No, no, little hen-sparrow – you can't trick me like that. I'm too clever."

He flew down to the crumbs and began to peck them up. The little hen-sparrow on the roof hopped up and down in the greatest excitement and fear. "Feathers! The cat is there! Come back, come back! Eat the crumbs later when the cat is gone!"

Feathers took no notice. He went on pecking up the crumbs, which were really delicious. That little hen-sparrow could be as clever as she liked – he wasn't going to take any notice.

But the hen-sparrow was not being clever – she was being kind. The cat really was there! And suddenly poor Feathers knew it, for there came a soft rustle – and the Persian cat pounced on the greedy little sparrow.

It would have been the end of Feathers if the little hen-sparrow on the roof hadn't made such a noise. Lucy, the little girl that the cat belonged to, heard the noise and came running out. Feathers flew off with almost no feathers in his tail.

Poor Feathers! It was a punishment for greediness and untruthfulness. He thought he was so clever – but he wasn't even clever enough to know that it is

foolish to be greedy and to tell untruths.

If you see a little sparrow with a rather short tail, have a look at him. It might be Feathers.

Do Hurry Up, Dinah!

Once upon a time there was a little girl called Dinah. She was pretty and had nice manners, and she was kind and generous.

But oh, how slow she was!

You should just have seen her dressing in the morning. She took about five minutes finding a sock. Then she took another five minutes putting it on. Then she spent another five minutes taking it off because it was inside out. By the time she was dressed and downstairs everyone else had finished breakfast.

At breakfast time she was just as slow. You really would have laughed to see her eating her porridge. First she sat staring at her plate. Then she put the sugar on very, very slowly and very, very carefully.

Then she stared at the plate again. Then she put on her milk. She stirred the porridge slowly round and round and round, and then she began to eat it.

She took quite half an hour to eat it, so she was always late for school. And, dear me, when she did get to school what a time she took taking off her coat and hat. What a time she was getting out her pencil and rubber and book! By the time that Dinah was ready to begin her work, the lesson was finished.

She had two names. One was Slow-coach, which her mother called her, and the other was Tortoise, which her teacher called her.

"Dinah, you should have been born a tortoise!" her teacher used to say. "You really should. You would have been quite happy as a slow old tortoise!"

"Well," said Dinah, "I wish I lived in Tortoise-town, wherever it is! I hate people always saying 'Do hurry up, Dinah, do hurry up, Dinah!' I'd like to live with tortoises. I'm sure they wouldn't keep hustling and bustling me like everyone else does."

Now it so happened that the wind changed at the very moment that Dinah said this. You know that many strange things are said to happen when the wind changes, don't you? Well, sometimes a wish will come true at the exact change of the wind – and that's what happened to Dinah!

Her wish came true. She suddenly found that everything round her went quite black, and she put out her hand to steady herself, for she felt giddy.

She caught hold of something and held on to it tightly. The blackness gradually faded, and Dinah blinked her eyes. She looked round, expecting to see the schoolroom and all the boys and girls sitting down doing writing.

But she didn't see that. She saw something most strange and peculiar – so peculiar that the little girl blinked her eyes in astonishment.

She was in a little village street! The sun shone down overhead, and around Dinah were funny little houses, with oval doors instead of oblong ones like ours.

She was holding on to something that was beginning to get very angry. "Let go!" said a slow, deep voice. "What's the matter? Let go, I say! Do you want to pull my shell off my back!"

Then, to Dinah's enormous surprise, she saw that she was holding tightly on to a tortoise as big as herself! He was standing on his hind legs, and he wore a blue coat, short yellow trousers, and a blue hat on his funny little wrinkled head.

Dinah stared at him in amazement. "Who are you?" she asked.

"I'm Mr Crawl," said the tortoise. "Will you let go, please?"

Dinah let go. She was so surprised and puzzled at finding herself in a strange village all of a sudden with a tortoise walking by, that she could hardly say a word. But at last she spoke again.

"Where am I?" she asked.

"In Tortoise-town," said the tortoise. "Dear me, I know you! You're the little girl that is called Tortoise at school, aren't you? You said you wanted to come here, didn't you – and here you are! Well, well – you'd better come home with me and my wife will look after you. Come along."

"I want to go home," said Dinah.

"You can't," said Mr Crawl. "Here you are and here you'll stay. No doubt about that. You should be pleased that your wish came true. Dear, dear, don't go so quickly. I can't possibly keep up with you!"

Dinah wasn't really going quickly. She always walked very slowly indeed – but the old tortoise shuffled along at the rate of about an inch a minute!

"Do hurry up!" said Dinah at last. "I can't walk as slowly as this. I really can't."

"My dear child, you were called Tortoise at school so you must be very,

very slow," said Mr Crawl. "Now, here we are at last. There's Mrs Crawl at the door."

It was all very astonishing to Dinah. She had passed many tortoises in the road, some big, some small, all wearing clothes, and talking slowly to one another in their deep voices. Even the boy and girl tortoises walked very slowly indeed. Not one of them ran!

Mrs Crawl came slowly to meet Dinah and Mr Crawl. She did not look at all astonished to see Dinah.

"This little girl has come to live in Tortoise-town," said Mr Crawl. "She needs somewhere to live, so I have brought her home."

"Welcome!" said Mrs Crawl, and patted Dinah on the back with a clawed foot. "I expect you are hungry, aren't you? We will soon have lunch! Can you smell it cooking?"

Dinah could and it smelled delicious. "Sit down and I will get lunch," said Mrs Crawl. Dinah sat down and watched Mrs Crawl get out a tablecloth.

It took her a long time to open the drawer. It took her even longer to shake out the cloth. It took her simply ages to lay it on the table! Then she began to lay the table with knives and forks and spoons. It took her over half an hour to do this and poor Dinah began to get more and more hungry.

"Let me put out the plates and glasses," she said impatiently, and jumped up. She bustled round the table, putting the things here and there. Mrs Crawl looked at her crossly.

"Now, for goodness sake don't go rushing about like that! It's bad for tortoises! It's no good getting out of breath and red in the face."

"I'm not a tortoise," said Dinah.

"Well, you soon will be when you have lived here a little while," said Mr Crawl, who had spent all this time taking off one boot and putting on one slipper. "You'll see – your hair will fall off and you'll be bald like us – and your neck will get wrinkled – and you'll grow a fine hard shell."

Dinah stared at him in dismay. "I don't want to grow into a tortoise!" she said. "I think you look awful."

Mr and Mrs Crawl gazed at Dinah in great annoyance. "Rude little girl," said Mrs Crawl. "Go and wash your hands. Mr Crawl will go and wash his first and show you where to run the water."

It took five minutes for Mr Crawl to walk to the washroom. It took him ten minutes to wash and dry himself, and by that time Mrs Crawl had actually got the lunch on the table. Dinah was so

hungry that she washed her hands more quickly than she had ever washed them in her life before!

Oh dear – what a long time Mr and Mrs Crawl took over their soup.

Dinah finished hers long before they were halfway through, and then had to sit and wait, feeling dreadfully hungry, whilst they finished. She fidgeted, and the two tortoises were cross.

"What an impatient child! Don't fidget so! Learn to be slower, for goodness sake! You wanted to come and live with us, didn't you? Well, be patient and slow and careful."

Lunch wasn't finished till four o'clock. "Almost teatime!" thought Dinah. "This is simply dreadful. I know now how horrid it must be for everyone when I am so slow at home or at school. They must feel as annoyed and impatient as I do now."

"I'll take you out for a walk when I'm ready," said Mrs Crawl. "There's a circus on in the marketplace, which perhaps you would like to see."

"Oh yes, I would!" cried Dinah. "Oh, do hurry up, Mrs Crawl. I'm sure that by the time you've got your bonnet on, and your shawl, the circus will have gone!"

"Nobody ever says 'Do hurry up!' in Tortoise-town," said Mrs Crawl, shocked. "We all take our own time over everything. It's good to be slow. We never run, we never do anything quickly at all. You must learn to be much, much slower, dear child."

It was six o'clock by the time that Mrs Crawl had got on her bonnet, changed her shoes and put on a nice shawl. Dinah thought that she had never in her life

seen anyone so slow. Sometimes Mrs Crawl would stop what she was doing, and sit and stare into the air for quite a long time.

"Don't dream!" cried Dinah. "Do hurry up!" And then she remembered how very, very often people had cried out the same thing to her, crossly and impatiently. "What a tiresome nuisance I must have been!" she thought. "Oh, dear – I didn't like hurrying up, but I hate even worse this having to be so slow!"

The circus was just closing down when they reached it. The roundabout was starting for the very last time. Dinah could have cried with disappointment. She got on to a horse, and the music began to play. The roundabout turned round very slowly indeed.

Dinah looked at all the creepy-crawly tortoises standing about, looking so solemn and slow, and she couldn't bear them.

"Oh, I wish I was back home!" she cried. "I wish I was! I'd never be slow again, never!"

The roundabout horse that she was riding suddenly neighed loudly. Dinah almost fell off in surprise. It turned its head and looked at her. "I'm a wishing-horse!" it said. "Didn't you know? Be careful what you wish!"

The roundabout went faster. It went very fast indeed. Then it slowed down and stopped – and hey presto, what a surprise! Dinah was no longer in Tortoise-town, but in a field at the bottom of her own garden! She knew it at once. She jumped off the horse and ran to the gate in her own garden wall. She looked back at the roundabout – and it slowly faded like smoke, and then it wasn't there any more.

Dinah tore up the garden path. She rushed down the passage to the kitchen. Her mother was there, and stared in amazement. She had never seen Dinah hurry herself before!

"What's happened to you?" she asked. "You're really being quick for once."

"I've been to Tortoise-town!" said Dinah. "And now I'm back again, hurrah! I'll never be a slow-coach or a tortoise again, never, never, never!"

She probably won't. Is there anyone you know that ought to go to Tortoise-town? Not you, I hope!

Jimmy and the
Elephant Man

Jimmy wanted to go to the circus. All his friends were going – but somehow his parents couldn't be bothered to take him. His mother wasn't very well and his father seemed very busy.

"I don't like to bother them," thought Jimmy. "They will only get cross with me. But how I wish I could go!"

"Jimmy! Jimmy! I want you to run an errand for me!" called Mother. "Hurry, now! Go to Mrs Brown and tell her I need twelve new-laid eggs tomorrow."

Jimmy put down his book and ran off. He went down the street, up the lane, over the hill, down to the farm, and all the way back again. It was a long walk, and Jimmy felt quite tired by the time he reached his own street once more.

Just as he turned into his street he saw an old lady sitting on a doorstep, crying! This was such a surprising sight that Jimmy stood still and stared for a moment, quite forgetting that it isn't kind to stare. But he didn't think that grown-ups ever cried.

"What's the matter?" he said to the old lady, going up to her. "Don't you feel well?"

"I've lost my purse with all my money in it," said the old woman, wiping her eyes with a big white handkerchief. "And there's my son's watch in it, too, which

has just been mended. He will be so cross with me!"

"Where do you think you lost your purse?" asked Jimmy, looking all round as if he expected to see it in the road somewhere.

"I've just come back from Mrs Brown at the farm," said the old lady. "I must have dropped it somewhere on the way."

"How funny!" said Jimmy. "I've just been to Mrs Brown's too – but I didn't see your purse on the way back. Of course, I was running, and not looking."

"I suppose you wouldn't go back and see if you can find it for me, little boy?" asked the old lady.

Jimmy didn't want to at all. He had already been all the way there and back, and he was tired and wanted to sit down with his book. It would be horrid to have to go to the farm again. But the old lady looked very sad, and he didn't like to think of someone as old as his granny sitting on a doorstep and crying like that.

"I'll go and find it for you," he said.

"You go home and sit down. I'll bring you the purse if I find it. Where do you live?"

"Number six, in the next street," said the old lady, getting up. "Thank you kindly, little boy."

She walked slowly down the street, and Jimmy went back down the lane, looking everywhere for the purse. He kicked up the leaves, he looked under the hedges – but he couldn't find that purse anywhere in the lane. He went up the hill and looked there. He went almost to the farm, hunting all the way – and just as he got to the first farm gate he saw the purse! It was a big brown one, lying in the mud! How pleased Jimmy was to see it!

He picked it up and ran off at once. His legs were really very tired by this time, but he felt so pleased about the purse that he didn't think of that!

He went to number six in the street next to his and knocked.

"Come in!" cried a voice. Jimmy went in. The old lady was sitting down by a

bright fire, drinking a cup of cocoa.

"I've found your purse!" said Jimmy, and he put it into her lap. "Wasn't that lucky!"

The old woman picked it up and opened it. She nodded her head. "Yes," she said, "all my money's there – and my son's watch too. Now, little boy, would you be so kind as to take this watch to my son for me? I'm too tired to go out again, and he wants it tonight."

Well, Jimmy thought that was too bad! To go out again! But never mind, he'd do it! He took the watch from the old lady, asked her where he was to take it and went out. Before he did anything more he ran home to tell his mother what had happened to him. She was getting quite worried about him.

"Well, Jimmy, you've been very kind to the old lady," she said. "Did she give you a reward to show she was grateful?"

"No, Mum," said Jimmy. "I expect she couldn't afford to give me anything – and anyway, I didn't want anything. I didn't like to see her crying."

He went off with the watch. He had to take it to a house not very far away. He knocked at the door and asked for Mr Siglio. That was the name of the old lady's son.

"He's upstairs," said the woman who opened the door. "You'll just catch him. He's off to his elephants in a minute!"

"His elephants!" said Jimmy, in surprise. "What do you mean?"

"Oh, he's the man that makes the elephants do their tricks at the circus," said the woman. "Didn't you know? Yes, he has eight fine elephants, and they all love him as if he were their brother! You should see how they twine their trunks round him and fuss him! Ah, you can see that man's been kind to his beasts!"

Mr Siglio sounded rather a nice man, Jimmy thought. He went up the stairs and knocked on another door. He went in and there was the famous Mr Siglio, dressing himself up in yellow trousers, a bright blue coat, and a great blue top hat, just as he appeared in the circus posters which were all over the town.

"Hello, hello!" said Mr Siglio, looking at Jimmy. "And who have we here? Mr Tickle-me-up – or Master Tumble-me-down?"

"No," said Jimmy. "My name's Jimmy, and I've brought you your watch. I saw your mother sitting on a doorstep and crying because she had lost her purse with her money in it and your watch too. I was lucky enough to find her purse and she asked me to bring you the watch. So here it is!"

"And very kind of you too," said Mr Siglio, taking the watch and stuffing it into his trousers pocket. "What can I do for you in return?"

"Oh, nothing, thank you," said Jimmy. "I hope your elephants perform well tonight."

"Have you seen them at the circus?" asked Mr Siglio.

"No," said Jimmy. "I haven't been, and I'm afraid I'm not going either."

"Bless us all!" said Mr Siglio, putting his blue top hat on his head, all on one side. "Here's a boy who hasn't seen my famous elephants! I can't allow this! Run home, boy, and tell your mother that Mr Siglio, the famous elephant man, wants you to help him at the circus tonight!"

100

So that night Jimmy went to the circus – and will you believe it, Mr Siglio got him into the big ring and made him help with the elephants. Yes, you could have seen Jimmy riding on one – and throwing

a ball to another – and giving a bun to a third! He had never had such an exciting time in his life!

"I didn't know that old lady's son was Mr Siglio, the famous elephant man," he told his father that night.

"Ah!" said his father, "there's a lot we don't know, Jimmy, till we give a bit of help to somebody. It's wonderful the things that happen then!"

When the
Moon Was Blue

One evening, when Jack and Mary were going to bed, they forgot to clean their teeth.

Their mother saw their toothbrushes lying beside their toothmugs and called to them:

"You naughty children! You haven't cleaned your teeth!"

"We forgot!" said Jack, and the two ran to get their brushes. "Have you ever forgotten to clean your teeth, Mummy?"

"Oh, I dare say I have," said Mummy.

"How often?" asked Mary.

"Oh, once in a blue moon!" said their mother, drawing the curtains back so that the air could come into the room.

"What's a blue moon?" said Jack.

"I really don't know," said Mother.

"Just an ordinary moon turned blue, I expect. I've never seen one."

"You often say things happen 'once in a blue moon'," said Mary. "But a blue moon never comes."

"Well – it might some day!" laughed Mother. "You'd better be careful then – for goodness knows what might happen if the moon turned blue!"

The children got into bed. Mother kissed them and said goodnight. Then she turned out the light and went downstairs.

"It's very light outside tonight," said Mary. "The moon must be up."

"Daddy said it would be a full moon tonight," said Jack. "Oh, Mary – wouldn't it be exciting if it was blue!"

"Yes – but it won't be," said Mary sleepily. "Things like that never seem to happen. Think how often we've tried to see fairies, and never have, and how often we've wished wishes and they haven't come true, and tried to work spells and they won't work. I don't believe in those things any more!"

"I still do," said Jack, "because once one of my wishes really did come true."

"Well, it must have been an accident, then," said Mary, yawning. "Goodnight, Jack. I'm going to sleep."

Both children fell fast asleep in a minute or two. They slept soundly, and didn't hear the wardrobe creaking loudly. They didn't hear the cat mewing outside.

But when twelve o'clock struck, they did hear something. At least, Jack did. He heard an owl hooting outside the window, and he opened his eyes.

"Wit-wit!" said the owl. "Woo-wit-wit!"

Jack sat up and wondered what time it was. He looked at the window. A good deal of light came in from outside, for the moon was full. It had gone behind a cloud for a moment, quite a small one, for Jack could see the moon behind it. He watched it, waiting for it to come out again.

And when it did he gasped and stared and rubbed his eyes – for what do you suppose? Why, the big round moon was as blue as forget-me-nots! There it shone in the sky, looking very peculiar indeed.

"There's a blue moon!" cried Jack. "Mary, Mary, wake up! There's a blue moon!"

Mary woke up with a jump and sat up. She stared at the moon in the greatest surprise.

"So there is!" she said "Oh, Jack – do you suppose anything extraordinary will happen? Oh, do let's go to the window and see if we can see any fairies or pixies about. Mummy said we might see them once in a blue moon!"

They ran to the window – and looked

down the moonlit garden. But not a fairy or pixie could they see.

"Let's wish a few wishes," said Jack, gazing up at the bright blue moon. "They might come true now the moon is blue."

"Yes, let's," said Mary. "I wish we could see a fairy or a gnome or something!"

"And I wish we could too!" said Jack.

And immediately they did! A gnome, very small and bent, ran out from under the lilac bush in the middle of the garden, and went to the little round pond. In the middle of this was a little statue of a rabbit, sitting on a big flat stone.

The gnome jumped over the water and landed beside the rabbit. At once the stone rabbit took his hand, and stood up. The gnome began to pull at the flat stone on which the rabbit had been sitting – and before the children's very eyes, he suddenly disappeared! The stone rabbit sat down again and made no more movement.

"Did you see that, Mary?" cried Jack. "Come on, quickly! We'll see where he disappeared to. Put on your dressing-gown and I'll put on mine."

They threw on their dressing-gowns and ran quietly down the stairs. Out they went into the garden and ran to the pond. With a leap Jack was over the water and standing beside the stone rabbit in the middle of the pond. To his enormous surprise, the small rabbit at once put a cold paw into his hand and got up. Jack turned to the flat stone – and saw an iron ring on it, just where the rabbit had sat. He pulled at it and the stone came up. Under it lay a steep stone stairway!

"Come on, Mary!" cried Jack. "Here's an adventure for us! We've always wanted one!"

Mary jumped over the water beside Jack and peered down the steps. The stone rabbit put its other paw into her hand, and looked beseechingly at her.

"This little rabbit's alive, although it's just a statue!" said Mary, in surprise. "Can you speak, Bunny?"

"Yes," said the rabbit. "I can speak,

once in a blue moon – and the moon is blue tonight!"

"Are you really a statue or are you alive?" asked Jack.

"I was once the first rabbit in the carriage of the Princess Philomela of Heyho Land," said the rabbit. "But one night the wicked gnome Twisty lay in wait for her carriage – and put a log in our path. So over I went and all the other three rabbits, and the Princess fell out of the carriage. The gnome picked her up and carried her off – and turned me and the other rabbits into stone. He sold us for the middles of ponds and there we stayed!"

"Goodness me!" said Jack, in the greatest surprise. "Whoever would have thought of such a thing? Where is the Princess now?"

"I don't know," said the rabbit, mournfully. "Still a prisoner somewhere, I expect. The gnome has a secret way to Fairyland down that stairway. He may have gone to the Princess now."

"Well, let's go after him then!" said Jack. "We may see where he keeps the Princess, and perhaps be able to rescue her! Will you come with us, Bunny?"

"Yes, but I'm made of stone, and I would make so much noise!" said the rabbit.

"I'll wish you alive again!" said Jack. "It seems as if wishes come true in a blue moon!"

"Yes, wish!" said Mary. So Jack wished hard.

"I wish this stone bunny may come alive!" he said, and immediately his wish came true! The little rabbit grew soft and warm and furry – and whiskers grew out of his cheeks. The stone rabbit had had no whiskers at all.

"I'm alive, I'm alive!" he cried, frisking round and nearly falling into the pond.

"Mind! You'll fall in the water!" said Mary, clutching hold of the excited bunny. "Come along. We'll go down the steps now."

So down the steps they all went, Jack first, then the bunny, then Mary. It was dark when they got to the bottom, but a lamp hung a little way farther on, and showed them a narrow passage. They went along, most excited.

After a while they came to a turnstile, and they pushed against it. It wouldn't turn round, and Jack thought they had better climb over it. But before he could do so a small brownie popped his head out of a window in the wall of the passage and said, "Penny each, please."

"We haven't any pennies," said Jack. "We are in our dressing-gowns, and we don't keep pennies there. Please let us through. Has the gnome Twisty gone this way?"

"Yes, he has," said the brownie,

nodding his head. "He often goes this way. No one else goes except myself – and I only go once in a blue moon!"

"Well, it's a blue moon tonight!" said Jack. "We've seen it!"

"What!" cried the brownie, his face full of excitement. "The moon is blue! My stars, I must go and look!"

He squeezed himself through the window in the wall of the passage, pushed past Jack, Mary and the rabbit, and disappeared up the tunnel.

"Come on, let's climb over, now he's gone!" said Mary. So they all climbed over the turnstile, and went on down the

tunnel again. But it didn't go very far this time. It opened out into a cave through which a dark, swift river ran. A little pixie sat by the side of some boats, half asleep.

"Wake up!" cried Jack, running to him. "Has the gnome Twisty gone this way?"

"Yes, down the river," said the pixie, in surprise. "But he said I was to let no one else but him have my boats today."

"Oh, well, it can't matter once in a blue moon!" said Jack, getting into one.

"What, is the moon blue?" cried the pixie, in delight. "Oh, have my boats then – have them all if you want to! I'm going up to see the moon, the moon, the moon!"

He sat down on a big toadstool growing near by and, to the children's great amazement, shot upwards at a great speed.

"Well, I suppose he's gone to see the moon, like the brownie," said Jack. "Come on, Mary and Bunny! We musn't let the gnome Twisty get too far ahead."

They set off in the boat. Jack steered,

but there was no need for oars, for the river was very strong and took them along itself. In a few minutes it came out into the open air, and there, hanging in the sky, was the moon, still as blue as forget-me-nots!

As the boat went along, Jack caught sight of a large notice on one of the banks. He looked at it. To his great surprise, it had one word on it:

JUMP!

"Jump," said Jack puzzled. "Why jump?"

"Oh, look!" cried Mary, pointing ahead. "There's a waterfall or something coming. Jack, if we don't jump, we shall go over the falls. Oh, I'm frightened!"

"Come with me," the rabbit said. He took the strings from Jack and steered the boat towards the bank. It ran into it with a bump, and at the same time all three jumped out! They landed on the

soft grass and rolled over. Just ahead of them the river shot over the falls with a roar. Their boat spun round once and then headed for the waterfall. Over it went, and that was the last they saw of it!

"Goodness! I hope this sort of thing only happens once in a blue moon!" said Jack.

"Oh, it does," said the rabbit. "Come on. Do you see that castle over there? I am sure that is where the gnome has gone. It belongs to him. Perhaps he has the Princess Philomela locked up in one of the rooms."

They all set off for the castle. They soon arrived there, and looked up at it. It was very big, and had hundreds of shining windows, and a great wooden door.

"I don't think I want to go in that door," said Mary. "It looks as if it might shut behind us and make us prisoners in the castle too. Isn't there another way of getting in?"

"We'll spy round and see," said Jack. So they walked all round the castle and right at the back they discovered a very small door, painted a bright yellow. Jack pushed it – and it came open!

He and the others peeped inside. It led into a great yard. They all went inside, and looked round. The kitchen door stood open and a smell of cakes being baked came out.

"Come on," said Jack. "We may be able to sneak inside."

He crept up to the kitchen door – and at that very moment a large gnome-woman came to it to shake a duster. She stared at the three in surprise. They didn't know what to say.

"Oh," she said at last, "I suppose you have come with a message for Twisty the gnome. You are not the washing, are you? Or the baker?"

"Oh, no," said Jack. "May we go inside and see the gnome?"

Mary was horrified to hear Jack ask this, for she certainly didn't want to see the horrid gnome Twisty, in case they were all taken prisoners. The gnome servant nodded her head.

"He's just upstairs with the Princess," she said. "But he won't be long. Come and wait in the hall."

She took them inside and led them to a great hall. They sat down on a bench and she disappeared back into the kitchen.

"Did you hear that?" said Jack, in excitement. "She said the gnome Twisty was upstairs with the Princess! So she is here! We'll rescue her! Come on – we must hide before the gnome comes back. I don't want to see him, of course – that was only an excuse to get inside!"

Jack, Mary and the rabbit looked

round to see where they could hide. There was a long curtain hanging at the foot of the stairs, and the three crept behind it. They hadn't been there more than a minute or two when they heard footsteps coming down the stairs. It was the gnome Twisty.

As he came into the hall, the gnome-woman ran out. "Master," she said, "there are three . . ."

She stopped short and looked round in surprise – for she could not see Mary, Jack or the rabbit. "How strange!" she said. "A boy and a girl and a rabbit came to see you. They were here just now!"

"Oh, indeed!" said Twisty, in a hoarse and threatening voice. "They were here, were they? Well, where are they now? I suppose you've let them go into my magic room, and disturb my spells. Grrrrrr! If you have, I'll turn you into a dustbin lid. That's all you're fit for!"

"Oh, Master, I don't think they've gone into your magic room!" cried the servant – but the gnome had disappeared into a little room on the opposite side of the

hall. The servant followed – and in a second Mary, Jack and the rabbit had slipped out from the curtain and were running upstairs as fast as they could!

At each landing they found locked doors. Jack stopped outside each one and called softly.

"Princess Philomela! Are you there?"

But there was no reply at all until he reached the topmost room of all – and then an answer came, in a soft, eager voice.

"Yes, yes! I am here! Who is it?"

The door was locked and bolted but the key was in the lock. Jack turned it, and then undid the bolts. He opened the door and saw inside the room a beautiful little princess with long golden hair waving round her face, and the brightest blue eyes he had ever seen.

"Oh, oh, you've come to rescue me!" cried Philomela, and she gave Jack and Mary a tight hug each. She saw the rabbit and clapped her hands in delight.

"Why, you are dear little Whiskers, one of the bunnies that used to pull my carriage!" she said, and she lifted him up and kissed him. "I suppose you

brought these children here to save me."

"We must go, Princess," said Jack. "The gnome knows we are here. He is looking for us downstairs. He may come up at any minute."

"Come along then," said Philomela.

So they all began to creep down the stairs and at last came to the hall. No one was there. Not a sound was to be heard. Every door that led into the hall was shut.

"I say!" said Jack. "I don't remember which door led into the kitchen, do you?"

"We don't need to go that way," said Mary. "What about trying the front door?"

"No," said Jack. "It's too big and heavy. It would make a noise. Let's go into one of the rooms, it doesn't matter which one so long at the gnome isn't there, and then climb out of the window. That should be easy."

So they listened outside the nearest door and, not hearing the tiniest sound from inside, they pushed open the door and slipped into the room. They ran to some curtains and pulled them aside to get at the windows – but alas – there were no windows at all!

Then they heard the sound of a key being turned in the lock – and looked round to see Twisty the gnome looking at them with a very nasty grin.

"Ha!" he said. "So you thought you would rescue the Princess and all escape very nicely, did you? Well, you made a mistake, I'm afraid. I have four prisoners now, instead of one!"

He went to the middle of the floor, and pulled up a small wooden trapdoor.

"Get down into my cellar," he said. "There is no escape from there. It is dark and cold and full of spiders. You will enjoy a night or two there, I am sure!"

The Princess and Mary began to cry. Jack looked fierce but could do nothing. The rabbit slipped down into the cellar without a word.

When they were all in the dark, damp cellar, the gnome shut the trapdoor with a bang and bolted it. They heard his footsteps going out of the room above.

"Oh dear! What are we to do?" sobbed Philomela. "Oh, I am so frightened."

"So am I!" said Mary, wiping her eyes.

"There's no need to be," said the rabbit, in a soft voice. "I can rescue you all. I am a bunny, you know, and my paws are good for digging holes. This cellar is in the ground; there is earth all around. It will not take me long to dig my way out and then I will fetch many more rabbits and we will all dig together."

"Splendid idea!" cried Jack. The rabbit at once began to scrape in the earth. Soon he had made quite a tunnel, and

the earth was piled in the cellar. In a few
minutes he had disappeared – and before
long he had fetched fifteen more rabbits,
who all dug and scraped away valiantly.

"Now I think the tunnel is big
enough," said the rabbit. And so it was.
Jack, Mary and Philomela easily made
their way up it, and came out at the side
of the big castle!

"The rabbits have brought a carriage
for you, Your Highness," said the little
rabbit – and there, sure enough, was a
shining silver carriage! Four rabbits stood
ready to pull it, and the Princess got in.

"You must come too," she said to the
children, but just as they were about to
get in, a peculiar thing happened.

"Look at the moon!" cried the rabbit,
and pointed to where the moon was
slowly sinking down in the sky.

Everyone looked. It was turning bright
yellow! Yes – there was no mistake about
it. All its blue colour was fading, and
even as they watched, it was all gone,
and there was the moon, as bright yellow
as a daffodil, filling the sky with light.

"The blue moon's gone," said the rabbit sadly. "It's gone – but we've rescued the Princess!"

A strange wind blew up at that moment and the children suddenly felt giddy. There came a loud humming noise. Jack and Mary sat down on the grass and shut their eyes, for they felt very peculiar.

After a while the humming noise died away and they opened their eyes.

Will you believe it? – they were back in their beds again! Yes, they were, both of them sitting up and gazing out of the window at the moon, which was yellow, and shining brightly!

"Mary!" cried Jack. "Did we dream it all?"

"No, we couldn't have," said Mary. "It was all so real. The moon really was blue!"

"Well, tomorrow we will look for that trapdoor again, where the bunny was," said Jack, lying down. "Then we will know for certain it was all true. How funny – Daddy will wonder where the stone bunny has gone, won't he?"

But do you know, when the morning came, the stone rabbit was back again. Yes, he was sitting in the middle of the pond on the big flat stone, just as before.

"But the trapdoor is underneath him, Daddy," said Mary, earnestly, after she had told her father all about their very strange adventure. "It really is. Will you take him off the stone and see?"

"No," said Father. "He is cemented to the stone. I'm not going to move him. You dreamed it all!"

Well, isn't that a pity? If only their father would move the rabbit and let the children find that trapdoor again, they would know it wasn't a dream. But he won't.

Perhaps you will see a blue moon one day. If you do, wish a wish – for it is sure to come true, once in a blue moon!

The Big Girl's Balloon

Once upon a time a little girl went to a party. It was a birthday party, and there were to be balloons and crackers. Sukie was looking forward to it.

"Now listen, Sukie," said her mother, as she dressed her for the party. "There will be a lot of big girls there, I expect, so you must try to be a big girl too, and not cry if you fall down or if you lose your chair at Musical Chairs."

"I'll try not to," said Sukie. "But, oh Mummy, I hope they don't have Blind Man's Buff and catch me! I might cry then!"

"Of course you won't," said her mother. "You don't want Geraldine to think you are a silly baby, do you?"

"Oh – is Geraldine going?" said Sukie,

pleased. Geraldine was a big girl who lived opposite. Sukie thought she was marvellous. She could ride a bicycle and a horse. She could run faster than anyone else. She had just won a scholarship at school. She went to the same dancing class as Sukie, and she was quite the best there.

"I like Geraldine," said Sukie. "She's a very clever girl, I think, Mummy – she's good at everything. And once at the dancing class she chose me for her partner."

"Well, that was very nice of her," said Mother, tying Sukie's hair with bright blue ribbons. "If there is dancing at the

party she might choose you again – but she certainly won't if you behave like a baby and cry if anything goes wrong."

"Well, I won't," said Sukie. "I promise you, Mummy, that I won't cry if I fall down, and I won't cry if I'm out first at Musical Chairs, and I won't cry if I'm caught at Blind Man's Buff. I always keep my promises to you, don't I?"

"You do, dear," said Mother. "So I know I can trust you not to cry for any of those things. It's not good to cry at somebody's birthday party, anyway – every moment should be happy for the birthday boy or girl."

Sukie went off to the party. They had tea almost as soon as she got there – and what a lovely tea it was. It began with buns and jam, and ended with the most enormous birthday cake Sukie had ever seen. It had nine candles on it, and little pink roses all round the edge in sugar.

After tea there were games and crackers. Sukie had two crackers and she pulled them with a little boy she knew. She wished Geraldine would pull

one with her but she was at the other side of the room.

Geraldine had seen Sukie and smiled at her. She was looking very grand indeed in a deep red velvet frock. Sukie thought she was the nicest girl there.

Geraldine won the Musical Chairs. As usual, Sukie was the first out, but she didn't cry at all. She stood aside and let the others go on playing, and, to her great delight, Geraldine won the game. She got a most beautiful big red balloon to match her frock.

Sukie thought it was the biggest and best she had ever seen.

After that every boy and girl was given a balloon to play with, but they were very much smaller than Geraldine's prize balloon.

Geraldine hung her red balloon high up on a picture so that it shouldn't pop. She played with her little one, like the others.

Bumping the balloons about all over the place was fun. Sukie had a pretty one. It was like a big green bubble. She liked it very much.

"It will be lovely to take it home with me, and hang it in my bedroom," she thought. "I shall look at it in the morning then."

But a dreadful thing happened almost as soon as she had thought that. Her balloon floated into the air, and came down on top of a sharp ornament on the bookshelf.

Pop! It burst. It was gone. There was nothing left of it but a little bit of dull green rubber.

Sukie was full of horror. Her balloon, her lovely green balloon, had burst. The

bang had made her jump – and when she saw that it was her balloon that had popped she was full of dismay.

"My balloon!" she said, and burst into tears.

A grown-up went to see if there were any more balloons left, but there weren't. Sukie sobbed bitterly. And then she saw Geraldine looking at her, and she felt terribly ashamed.

"I cried at a birthday party," she thought, and turned away. "I was a baby in front of Geraldine. Oh, I do feel so ashamed of myself. I promised Mummy I wouldn't cry if I fell down, or was out in Musical Chairs, or got caught at Blind Man's Buff – but I've cried for something else. And Geraldine will think I'm such a baby. She'll laugh at me. She'll never ask me to dance with her again."

She went away into a corner to dry her eyes. The others were playing a game of General Post. Geraldine was playing it, too. But soon Geraldine slipped out of her place and went to Sukie.

"Sukie, come and play," she said. "Sukie, look what I've brought you!"

Sukie looked – and looked again. Geraldine was holding out to her her lovely red balloon, the one she had got as a prize.

"Oh, Geraldine, but that's your prize," said Sukie. "Oh, I'm sorry I cried. You must have thought I was dreadful."

"Shall I tell you a secret?" said Geraldine. "Well, when I was older than you I went to a Christmas party – and my balloon burst too – just like yours. And I cried ever so much louder than you did.

So I know just how you feel, you see.
And someone was so nice to me – they
gave me their balloon. So I thought if
ever I had a chance I'd do the same to
somebody else."

"Oh, you are a kind girl," said Sukie, suddenly feeling very happy. "But I couldn't take your prize balloon. Did you really cry like me at that Christmas party?"

"Much, much worse," said Geraldine. "I had to be taken home, and my mother was so ashamed of me. Now, take my balloon and come and play. And if ever you see somebody crying because their balloon has gone pop, well, you do what I did, and tell them how you cried once, and give them your own balloon!"

"Oh, I will – I will!" said Sukie; and she took the red balloon and went back to play. She felt very happy. Geraldine didn't think she was a baby – and she had given her her lovely balloon. She could have danced for joy.

And now, at every party she goes to Sukie is watching for somebody to burst their balloon and cry. She knows what she is going to do then. I'd rather like to do it, too, wouldn't you?

The Fish That
Got Away

"Look!" said Stella, suddenly, sitting up straight. "Look – there's a boy throwing stones at those seagulls!"

The others uncurled themselves from the warm sand on the beach and sat up to look. Sure enough, they saw a big boy throwing stones at a group of seagulls at the edge of the sea.

"He'll have to be stopped," said Peter, but he didn't do anything about it.

"He nearly hit one of them," said Jean. "The beast. Peter, go and stop him."

But the boy throwing stones was much bigger than Peter. Peter didn't move. It was John that got up in a hurry and ran yelling down the beach.

John was smaller than Peter, but he had a very loud voice. You should have heard him shouting at the boy.

"Hey you! Stop that! Throwing stones at birds is NOT allowed! STOP THAT!"

And would you believe it, the boy stopped throwing stones at once, and ran off. He saw everyone on the beach sitting up and staring, and he was ashamed and afraid.

"One of those gulls is hurt, I think," said Jean, and she got up. "Good old John – he's the smallest of us all, and yet he was the bravest. You're a coward, Peter."

"Same to you," said Peter, at once. "You're my twin, aren't you? Why couldn't you have gone and shouted?"

"Well, I'm a girl," said Jean. "It's boys who should do things like that."

"That's right – make excuses for yourself," Peter said sulkily. He didn't get up to join Jean as she went down the beach to John. Nor did Stella. But Stella was the most ashamed! Oh, dear – why had she let John go shouting at that boy all by himself? She ought to have gone with him.

John had gone to the seagull. The others had flown off, but this one stood looking rather dazed. It moved away a little as John got up to it, but didn't fly.

"It's just stunned by a stone, I think," said John, going carefully up to it. "Look, Jean, its wing is hurt. I wonder if we could take it home and look after it for a day or two till it recovers. It doesn't seem very badly hurt."

The gull let John pick it up. Jean was afraid of the big bird and wouldn't touch it, but Stella came running down to help.

"You were brave, John," she said. "I should have come with you and shouted, too."

"You needn't worry! I can manage things like that by myself," said John. "Anyway, bullies like that boy are always cowards – they run away at once! Help me with this gull, Stella."

The gull stayed quietly under John's arm till he reached home. Its eyes were half-shut. It seemed quite dazed.

Mother was very sorry to hear all about it. She bathed its wing, and then told John to take the gull into the garden and put it into the shed, so that it could keep quiet till it felt better.

"Leave the door open," she said. "Then it will not feel it is a prisoner. It can go out when it wants to."

Well, just as the children were sitting down to their tea, they heard the sound of a loud seagull cry: "EE-ew, EE-ew!" Then they heard the flap of wings. They looked up. Standing on the window-ledge was the gull, its eyes wide open now, looking at them.

"Ee-ew," said the gull, more quietly, and then it spread its great grey wings and flew off into the sky.

"Well! It came to say thank you!" said Stella. "It's better now. I'm so glad."

Everyone was glad. When they went out after tea they went down to the rocks to see if they could make out the gull they had helped. But they couldn't.

"They all look so alike when they are in a bunch together," said Jean. "First I think it's this one, then I think it's that one – I just can't be sure."

No gull came flying down to them, as John half hoped. He thought it would be very nice to have a friendly gull walking round them. But all the birds kept together, and not one gull even looked at the four children.

They walked home by the pier. Peter saw a big notice up. He went over to look at it. Then he called the others.

"I say – look! There's a fishing competition on the pier tomorrow – a prize for the biggest and best fish caught – children under twelve. Well, we're all under twelve. Let's go in for it. You just never know, we might be lucky and catch a big fish."

"Yes – let's," said Jean, who liked fishing with a line off the pier. "I'm sure Mummy will let us."

Their mother was only too glad to say she would pack up sandwiches and cake, and let them join the competitors in the fishing on the pier. "Dear me – how wonderful to get rid of you all for a whole day!" she said, with a twinkle in her eye. "Now I can go and see Granny."

About twenty children crowded on to the pier the next day, armed with fishing-rods or lines, and plenty of bait. They all went to look at the prizes – first, second, and third.

The first prize was a big book on ships. "Hope none of us wins that," said Stella. "We've got that book already."

"The second prize is that shrimping

net," said Peter. "I'd like that. It's a very fine one."

The third prize was a beach ball, a nice one. But the four children didn't particularly want that, either, because they already had a very nice one themselves.

"We'll have to hope to win the second prize," said Peter. "Bags I do!"

"Bags you don't!" said a boy near him, and Peter grinned.

"Hello, Ken – you in for the competition too? I hope we all get some good fish."

"My dad says we won't," said Ken, who was a fisherman's son. "He says the wind's not right today for fishing off the pier. He says we'll be lucky if we even get a good-sized mackerel! We'll only get tiddly little dabs."

Well, it was great fun going in for the competition. Peter, John, Jean and Stella all chose good positions and let down their baited lines. They had no fishing-rods, but they considered lines were just as good.

The competition began at twelve. Not one of the twenty children had caught a fish by the time it was one o'clock. It was very disappointing.

They called a halt to their fishing while they gathered together and ate sandwiches and cake and talked. Most of the children knew one another, and it was fun.

At two o'clock they all began fishing again. Ken got the first bite. He hauled up his line in glee. Then he gave a shout of disgust. "A crab! Look at that! Back you go, crab, I don't want you."

Back went the crab just as Peter gave a shout. He had felt something pulling at his bait. He hauled up the line but it was only a tiny little dab wriggling on the hook. That wouldn't win any prize at all.

It was rather a slow afternoon, because, as Ken's father had said, the wind was not right for fishing off the pier. One or two more dabs were caught, and a peculiar fish that nobody knew the name of. Two more crabs were caught and thrown back.

Then John caught a fish. He felt the sudden big tug at his line and sat up at once. "I've got one!" he called in excitement. "And a big one, too. My word, he's pulling!"

He hauled up his line. Everyone waited breathlessly to see what fish would come swinging and wriggling out of the water.

"It's a cod! My word, quite a big one!" yelled John in delight.

"You'll win the prize!" called the children.

"It's a beauty!" said Ken. "You are lucky!"

"Isn't he struggling hard?" said Jean. "I hope the line doesn't break, John."

It didn't – but just as John was carefully pulling the fish up to the pier-side, something happened. The fish gave a sudden strong flap, and somehow or other got off the hook. It fell downwards to the sea with a splash, gave a flick of its tail, and disappeared.

Loud groans came from everyone. The pier-master, hearing all the excitement, came up.

"Hello – anyone caught a real fish at last?" he said.

"It got away," said John , dolefully. "It was very big, indeed, Mr Wills. As big as this!" And he stretched out his arms.

"My word, was it?" said Mr Wills. "Well, well – it's always the biggest ones that get away, you know. Better luck next time."

"Bad luck, John," said Ken. "You really deserved the prize for that fish. In fact, I think you ought to get it, even though it got away. Nobody will catch a fish half that size!"

They all went on fishing. Ken caught a plaice, the biggest fish yet, though not half as big as the one that had got away. He put it proudly into his basket.

Then somebody caught a small cod, a codling, but it wasn't as big as Ken's plaice.

Ken suddenly gave a groan. "Look at those gulls – they've settled on the water round the pier, and now they'll get the fish, not us. Blow them!"

The gulls bobbed up and down, and

two or three of them dived in for fish. It really was annoying for the children, but, still, it was almost teatime now, and the competition was nearly over.

The pier-master came up again. "Time!" he said. "Put your fish into your baskets, please, and come to the scales to weigh them. Anyone with tiny fish needn't bother – I can see one or two good plaice and a codling, anyway."

"Oh, I do wish I'd caught that fish that got away," said John, pulling in his line. "Ah, look – here comes the steamer!"

The gulls all rose up into the air as the steamer approached, sounding its siren. One of the gulls flew over the pier. As it flew over, something fell from its beak right at John's feet, making him jump.

It was a large mackerel! John stared in

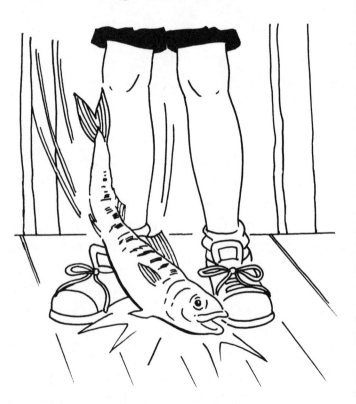

amazement and then looked up at the gull, which had now flown off. What a lovely big fish! But could he put it in for the competition? He hadn't caught it.

The others crowded round. "Yes, you put it in," they said. "You caught a much bigger one that got away. And anyway, the mackerel has been caught, and given to you by the gull. It's yours!"

"Yes – we'll let you give it in!" said Ken. They all liked John. "You had a piece of bad luck – now you've got some good luck!"

"No, I shan't put it in," said John. "It wouldn't be fair. But thanks all the same." He went with the others to see the fish weighed. Ken's plaice was the heaviest. Then came the codling, and a large dab. The pier-master suddenly caught sight of John's mackerel.

"Here – wait a minute! There's another big fish here," he said, and took it out of John's basket. He swung it on to the scales. "Why, it's second best," he said. "You've won second prize, John!"

"No, I haven't really," said John, and

he told the pier-master the story of the gull and how it had dropped the mackerel at his feet.

Stella suddenly interrupted. "John! John! Do you know, I believe it must have been that gull you saved yesterday – when you made that boy run – the one who was throwing stones! It must have been the very same gull!"

Well, everyone thought the same. "How extraordinary," said Ken. "Well, you'll have to have second prize, John – you deserve it."

"No, thanks," said John. "I didn't catch the fish, as you all know very well."

"Now, I'm the judge of this competition," said the pier-master, "and what I say goes. There shall be two second prizes, exactly the same – one for the mackerel, and one for the codling. I'll get another shrimping net. Is that all right, everyone?"

"YES!" yelled everybody, and John grinned in delight. The pier-master went to his store cupboard and brought out another net. "Here you are, John," he

said. "Share it with the gull, if you like –
but we all think it's fair to give you a
prize!"

Everyone cheered. John went off with
Stella, Jean and Peter, glowing with
pleasure. Overhead a gull soared, and
the four children heard its laughing cry:

"EE-ew, EE-ew, EE-ew!"

"I bet that's our gull," said Jean. "He's
glad you got the prize. And so am I."

The children's mother said it couldn't
have been the same gull, it was just a
bit of luck that one had let its fish fall
near John. I don't know what to think.
What do you think? Whatever anyone
says, it seems right that the fish should
have gone to John, doesn't it?

The
Astonishing Party

All the children in Hawthorne Village were excited. They had been invited to a party. And Dame Twinkle was giving it! Dame Twinkle was a marvellous person, as magic as can be. She knew all kinds of tricks and jokes and spells. She could tell you what the weather would be on Wednesday week. She could tell you where to find the first violet and the biggest bluebell. She knew where the juiciest blackberries grew and the finest nuts.

She was jolly and friendly and amusing – and how she could scold if she was cross! It would be exciting to go to a party given by Dame Twinkle.

"You'll have to behave yourselves," said Miss Brown, their teacher. "Dame

Twinkle doesn't like naughty or ill-mannered children, so be careful!"

Well, the children all dressed themselves up nicely and went up the hill to Dame Twinkle's cottage. Its windows were like her name – they twinkled in the sun, and the garden was bright with flowers. It was a sunny day, so the children hoped they could play in the garden.

Dame Twinkle welcomed them. "Good afternoon, Amy – and Benny – and Connie – and Dick – and Elaine and all of you! How nice you look!"

"I hope she's got a good tea!" whispered Patrick to Connie. Dame Twinkle had sharp ears and she heard what Patrick said. She frowned.

"Now," she said, "this will be rather a funny party, so be careful how you behave. There is a good bit of magic about the garden this afternoon!"

First of all Dame Twinkle gave the children coloured balloons to play with. That was fun! They threw them into the air, punched them when they came down again, and had a lovely time.

Then Gloria threw her balloon too near a holly bush – and it caught on a prickle and burst. Gloria burst too – into tears! She sobbed and she wailed, and Dame Twinkle came running up in alarm.

"My dear child, what have you done – broken a leg or an arm?"

"My balloon's burst!" wailed Gloria.

"Now, my dear, you are behaving like a little goose," said Dame Twinkle, firmly. And then a very strange thing happened.

Gloria turned into a goose! She did, really. She still wore her own clothes,

CACKLE
CACKLE

but she was a goose. She opened her beak
to wail, but she cackled instead.

"Oh – it's the magic in the garden!"
cried the children, in delight. "Oh, Dame
Twinkle, Gloria behaved like a goose and
she is one! Goosie-goosie-Gloria!"

"Well, well – you can't say I didn't
warn you!" said Dame Twinkle. "Cheer
up, Gloria, the magic will go sooner or
later!"

"Dame Twinkle, do you like the
beautiful dress my aunty gave me?" said
Polly, a very vain little girl, running up to
Dame Twinkle. She twisted herself round
to show the dress.

"My!" said Dame Twinkle. "You're as proud as a peacock, Polly, aren't you!"

And dear me, Polly changed into a peacock! There she stood, dressed in her clothes still, but with a magnificent tail spread out behind her – a very fine peacock indeed. She opened her beak to cry, but made an ugly screeching noise instead.

Micky stared, afraid. He ran into a corner, and tried to hide. He was always afraid of everything. Elaine pointed her finger at him. "Look at Micky! He's as timid as a mouse!"

And Micky at once turned into a mouse, of course – a nice big one, dressed in shorts and jersey, with a woffly nose, and a long tail. He had to carry it because he fell over it. He squeaked when he wanted to talk.

"I say – we'd better be careful," said Bobbie in alarm. "There's an awful lot of magic about today!"

"Come and have tea, come and have tea!" cried Dame Twinkle, and the children rushed indoors. They saw such a fine tea, and Patrick's eyes gleamed. He was a very greedy little boy. He sat himself down opposite the biggest plate of buns.

How he ate! He stuffed himself full of buns and sandwiches, cakes and biscuits, and the other children stared at him in disgust.

"You're as greedy as a pig, Patrick," said Bobby. And dear me – Patrick was immediately a pig! There he sat, grunting, his little piggy eyes staring all round, and his curly tail sticking out at the back of him. The children laughed.

Patrick really did look very funny.

The children were told to help themselves, and they did – all except Dick, who waited to be asked. Nobody asked him what he wanted, of course, and he felt very hurt, and sat with his plate empty for a long time.

He saw all the other children eating the things he liked. Soon his eyes filled with tears and he cried.

"What's the matter?" said Dame Twinkle. "Do you feel ill, Dick?"

"No. But oh, nobody looks after me, nobody offers me anything, and I've had hardly any tea!" wailed Dick.

"Well, didn't I tell you all to help yourselves?" said Dame Twinkle, impatiently. "You *are* a little donkey!"

And he was – a dear little grey donkey, with big, long ears that twitched, and a voice that said "Hee-haw!" very loudly! The other children laughed and petted him.

"Shall I get you some thistles and carrots for your tea?" said John. "Dear little Dickie Donkey!"

Martin slipped away from the table and went into the field beyond the garden. He came back with an armful of thistles which he pushed under poor Dick's nose.

"Now, Martin, now," said Dame Twinkle, "you really are a monkey to go and get those thistles!"

And of course, as soon as she said that, Martin was a monkey with a grinning face, and a long tail that was very useful to him, for he at once jumped up to the lamp, and hung downwards from it by his tail!

The children squealed. What an astonishing party! Who would change next? Really, it was so sudden, you never knew what your neighbour was going to turn into from one minute to the next.

Frank pushed some food into his pocket, hoping that no one would see him. Then he could eat cakes and biscuits in bed that night. But Dame Twinkle's sharp eyes did see him. She pounced on him at once!

"Now Frank, you take those things out of your pocket at once! None of your artful ways here! You're as sly as a fox, the way you behave!"

And a fox he was, a beautiful red fox, with a pointed nose, sharp ears and a wonderful tail. The children looked at him.

"Well – Frank always was a bit like a fox!" said Pam. "He had such a sharp nose, hadn't he!"

"Really, this party seems to be turning into a zoo!" said Dame Twinkle, looking round at the birds and animals there. "There are only a few of you left that

164

are boys and girls. Well, well, well!"

She started them off on a hopping race round the garden, while she went to wash up the tea-things. Hop-hop-hop they went down the path.

"Fanny's cheating!" cried Annie. "She put her other foot to the ground."

"You're cheating yourself!" cried John. "Look at you – two feet on the ground now!"

"So are you, John!" said Benny, and he gave him a push. John pushed back. The other children hopped quickly ahead. The boys rushed after them to stop them.

"Begin again, begin again!" cried Annie. "It's not fair! Benny, don't tug at my frock. You'll tear it."

John smacked Benny, and he hit John back. "You look as cross as a bear!" he said. And Benny became a bear – a nice, soft fat little bear, with tears rolling down its nose because John had hit it. He opened his big mouth to wail, but only a grunt came out.

Then the children began to quarrel again about who had won the hopping race. Annie knocked Elaine over. John pushed Annie. They screamed and behaved very badly indeed.

Dame Twinkle came running out, looking cross. Couldn't these children amuse themselves even for ten minutes without squealing and fighting?

"Now, now!" she cried. "Stop fighting like cats and dogs! I'm ashamed of you!"

Well! All those who were squabbling at once became cats and dogs – and there they were, tails swinging or wagging, voices mewing or barking, a most astonished lot of creatures!

Dame Twinkle looked at them all. "A goose – a donkey – a mouse – a peacock – a pig – a fox – a monkey – a bear – and any amount of cats and dogs!" she said. "What a party! Well, I meant this to be a children's party, not a zoo meeting. You'd better all go home, and I'll save the supper lemonade and biscuits till tomorrow morning. Then, if you are nicely-behaved boys and girls again, you can come and get them."

So the donkey, the goose, the mouse, the peacock, the fox, the pig, the monkey, the bear and the cats and dogs all went rather sadly home, wondering what their mothers would say when they saw them.

But you will be glad to know that as soon as they reached their own gates they turned back into boys and girls again, much to their delight. So maybe they will get the lemonade and biscuits tomorrow after all.

What an astonishing party! Do you think you would have turned into a bird or animal if you had been there? And if so – what would you have been?

The
Peculiar Bicycle

Christmas was over. The only party that Jane and Donald had been asked to was over as well. They had spent their Christmas money, but they hadn't been given much that year.

"And now we've got to wait ages for our birthdays to come," said Jane. "No more excitement, no more presents, no more parties for weeks and weeks and weeks."

Then they saw the big posters about the circus. *Galliano's Circus*, said the posters. *The most wonderful circus in the world. Clowns, horses, bears, elephants, acrobats – come and see them!*

They rushed home to their mother. "The circus is coming!" they shouted. "Can we go?"

"Yes, if you try to be good and helpful," said their mother. "But mind – one really naughty thing and you won't go!"

"We'll be as good as gold!" promised the children. And so they were until one afternoon when they went to play in the garden. Donald couldn't find the soft tennis ball, so he took his cricket ball – and that was forbidden in their small garden because there were so many windows all round. Not only their own windows, but other people's as well.

"Mum's out – she won't know we're playing with a hard ball," said Donald, swinging his bat. "Come on – bowl to me, Jane."

"Well, for goodness sake hit the ball down the garden to the fence, not to the right or left," said Jane, and she bowled to Donald. *Smack!* He hit the ball straight down the garden and Jane stopped it neatly. But the fourth ball was such a lovely easy one that Donald hit out with all his might, much harder than he meant to.

Crash!

The ball had sailed high in the air, and had gone straight for a window of the house at the bottom of the garden. It smashed into a pane of glass with a terrific noise and disappeared into the room beyond. The children stood still, staring in horror.

"That's Mr Screw's house – and the ball has smashed the window of his workroom," said Donald. "He will be angry!"

He certainly was! He came raging out of his house, shouting at the top of his

voice. "Who did that? Who broke my window?"

"We did," said Donald, in rather a shaky voice. "I'm so sorry, Mr Screw."

"Being sorry won't mend my window," said Mr Screw. "That ball has done other damage, too – it smashed my clock that was standing on a table nearby. It's broken! You'll have to pay for those two things – my clock and my window. Ah! Some of your Christmas money will have to go to that."

"We haven't any," said Jane, trembling at Mr Screw's angry voice. "We spent it all. We haven't any in our money-boxes either. We spent all that on Christmas presents."

"Well, what are you going to do then?" demanded Mr Screw. "I'm not paying for the window and the clock. I shall complain to your mother. Fancy letting you play with a hard cricket ball when there are windows all round!"

"Don't tell our mother," begged Jane, remembering that they might not be allowed to go to the circus. But Mr Screw did tell their mother. He went round and complained that very evening. Mother was very cross.

"You know what I said – no going to the circus if you were naughty," she said. "And what are you going to do to pay for a new window and clock for Mr Screw?"

The children didn't know. Jane was crying. Why, oh why, had they disobeyed their mother and used that hard ball?

Mr Screw poked Donald in the chest. "Now, you listen to me. The boy I use for my errands and little jobs is ill. You and this girl can take his place for a week, see? And that will make up for the broken window and clock. But mind, I'll work you hard!"

Mother said they must go and do what Mr Screw wanted. "And mind you do everything cheerfully and well," she said. "No sulking or shirking."

So they went the next day to see what errands Mr Screw wanted done. He was a carpenter, and made and mended all kinds of things in his little workroom. Donald and Jane had to fetch broken chairs and stools, and deliver them again when they were mended. They had to help Mr Screw with his work, too.

"Hold this, boy, while I glue it properly," Mr Screw would say. "Here, girl – pop the glue-pot on the fire again.

Quickly! Look alive! And just sweep up all these shavings on the floor. Put them in that box over there. I use them for lighting my fire in the morning."

He was a cross, peevish old man.

He never once said thank you. He never once gave them a biscuit or a sweet. He grumbled and groaned all the time, and the two children wished and wished the week would come to an end.

"I'm sorry for you," Mother said. "But you have to realise that if you do silly or wrong things they have got to be paid for somehow. Anyway, I'm glad to see you are nice and cheerful about it. I think you're doing your best. It's a pity Mr Screw isn't nicer to you, but it is your fault you're having to work for him!"

Saturday came at last. The last day of their work for Mr Screw – and oh dear, what a pity, the last day of the circus too!

"I should think everyone has seen it but us," Donald said gloomily. "Jack's seen it three times! Bother Mr Screw – why did he have to have a window right in the way of our ball?"

Mr Screw was at work on something very strange when they went to him that day. The children stared at it. It was a bicycle – but what a very peculiar one! It was made of wood that was jointed here, there and everywhere, so that if anyone rode it it jerked and wobbled and went into all kind of peculiar shapes!

"I've just finished mending it," said Mr Screw. "It belongs to my son. It got its handle broken last night but I've made a good job of it now. Just wants a lick of paint, that's all."

He stared at it and then looked at the children. "See that tin of paint over there? Well, you can do the painting. Red handlebars and mudguards. Set to work!"

That was rather a nice job. The children painted hard, and made the curious bicycle look very nice. Mr Screw grunted.

"Finished? All right, that's all I want you to do, just now – but I want you to come back at two o'clock and deliver it to my son. The paint will be dry then. Don't forget – two o'clock. That's your last job. And I hope you'll have learned your lesson by then, and not go round breaking people's windows and clocks any more!"

"He really is a very cross old man," said Donald to Jane, as they went home. "I only hope his son isn't as cross. Whatever does he want such a very peculiar bicycle for?"

At two o'clock they went round to Mr Screw's again to get the bicycle.

"There it is. The paint's dry now," said Mr Screw. "Take it to the Town Hall, go

to the big door at the back, and ask for Screwy the clown."

The children stared in astonishment. Screwy the clown? Why, his name was on all the circus posters – and yes – of course! He was shown riding a very odd bicycle. This must be his bicycle! No wonder it was so peculiar, all joints and knobbles and squeaks. It was a clown's bicycle!

They wheeled the bicycle away without a word. Mr Screw watched them go. He didn't thank them for what they had done for him that week. He didn't even give them any money. He was glad he had punished them, and made them do so much work for nothing.

"How strange that Mr Screw the carpenter should have a son called Screwy the clown!" said Jane. "Oh, dear – I do hope Screwy isn't as horrid as his father!"

They took the bicycle to the big door at the back of the Town Hall. A man was there, guarding the door. "Who do you want?" he asked.

"Screwy the clown, please," said Donald. "We have brought back his bicycle. It's mended."

The Town Hall seemed quite different when they took the bicycle in to find Screwy. People rushed about all over the place. Part of the back had been turned into stables. An elephant peeped over a wire fence at them. Music sounded somewhere in the distance.

Someone came rushing up to them. It was a clown with a white face, red nose, red lips, enormous false ears and great black eyebrows. He was in clown's dress, and hat, and he wore simply enormous shoes that flapped as he walked.

"Hey, there! That's my bike! Did you bring it?"

"Oh – are you Screwy the clown?" asked Donald. "Yes – your bike's mended. I do so wish I could see you ride it – it's a crazy bike!"

"Haven't you been to the show and seen me ride my bike?" said Screwy, astonished. "Aren't you allowed to come to the circus?"

"Well – we were going – but we broke your father's window and clock, and Mum said we couldn't go," said Donald. "We've been working for your father all the week to help pay for what we broke."

"Oh – you're the kids he told me about!" said Screwy. "Well, well! He told me he'd never had such a fine pair of workers – quick and cheerful and never a moan or a grumble! But I bet the old man didn't give you a kind word or any money! He's like that, is my dad, always has been. But he's not bad at heart – just grumpy and grumbly. Thanks for helping him."

Screwy suddenly got on his ridiculous bike and wobbled past them, swinging

strangely and swaying and jolting on the jointed machine. The children roared with laughter. He jumped off and called to someone nearby.

"Hey, Jimmy! These kids are friends of my dad's. They've worked for him all the week. Give them four tickets for our last show tonight, will you? Front row and all!"

And before Jane and Donald could say a word, Jimmy had pressed four red tickets into their hands, and he and Screwy had gone off together at top speed on the crazy wooden bicycle!

"Gracious!" said Jane, her face suddenly bright red. "Tickets for the circus. Four, Donald!"

"Dad and Mum can come, too!" shouted Donald. "Come on – let's get back and tell them. Four seats in the front row. I say! It can't be true."

But it was, of course – and tonight Jane, Donald, their mother and their father will all be sitting in the very front row of the ring, waiting for the circus to begin.

Do you know who they're going to clap loudest of all? Yes – you're right! Screwy the clown and his most peculiar bicycle, of course.

Chinky
Takes a Parcel

Chinky was doing his shopping in the pixie market. It was full today, and there were a great many people to talk to. Chinky was a chatterbox, so he loved talking.

His shopping-bag was full. He had no more money to spend. It was getting near his lunch time. "I really must go home," said Chinky, and he picked up his bag.

"Hey!" called Sally Simple. "Did you say you were going home? Well, will you deliver this parcel to Mrs Flip next door to you? It's for her party this afternoon."

"Certainly," said Chinky, and he took the parcel, which felt very cold indeed to him.

"You are sure you are going straight home?" Sally Simple asked anxiously. "I don't want you to take the parcel unless you are really off home now."

"I'm going this very minute," said Chinky. "Goodbye!"

He set off home – but he hadn't gone far before he met Dame Giggle, and she had a funny story to tell him. He listened and laughed, and then he thought of a much funnier story to tell Dame Giggle.

So it was quite ten minutes before he set off home again – and then whom should he meet but Old Man Grumble, who stopped him and shook hands.

Chinky hadn't seen Old Man Grumble for a long time and he had a lot of news to tell him. He talked and he talked, and Old Man Grumble hadn't even time to get one grumble in!

"You are a chatterbox, Chinky," he said at last. "Goodbye! Perhaps you'll let me get a word in when next we meet."

Chinky set off again. The cold parcel that he was carrying for Sally Simple seemed to have got very soft and squashy now. It was no longer cold either. It was rather warm and sticky.

"Goodness! I wonder what's in this parcel," thought Chinky, hugging it under his arm. A little drop of creamy liquid ran out of one corner and dripped down Chinky's leg. It was ice cream in the parcel, a big yellow brick of it, which Mrs Flip had ordered for her party. She was going to put it into her freezer when she got it, and then it would keep cold and icy till four o'clock.

Chinky went on his way, humming. Some more ice cream melted and ran down his leg. Chinky didn't know. He

was nodding excitedly at little Fairy Long-Wings, who was standing at her gate.

"Hello, Long-Wings!" called Chinky. "Glad to see you back. How did you enjoy your holiday?" And, dear me, he stood talking at Long-Wings' gate for ten minutes. Long-Wings didn't tell him a word about her holiday, for Chinky was so busy chattering about himself and his garden and his shopping. And all the time the ice cream dripped down his legs.

Well, when at last he arrived at Mrs Flip's, the box was almost flat and empty. He handed it to Mrs Flip and she looked at it in dismay.

"My ice cream for the party!" she cried. "It's all melted! Look at your legs, Chinky – what a mess they are in! Well, really, you might have brought it to me at once! I suppose Sally Simple gave it to you, thinking that you were coming straight home!"

"Well, so I did!" Chinky replied indignantly. "I came straight home, as straight as could be!"

"I don't believe you," said Mrs Flip. "I know you, Chinky, you're the worst chatterbox in town! Oh yes! You met Mr So-and-So, and you talked to him for ages and you saw Mrs This-and-That, and you chattered for ten minutes and you came across Dame Such-and-Such and you had a good long talk! And all the time my ice cream was melting. Take it! I don't want it now – it's just an empty box."

She threw it at Chinky and it hit him

on the nose. He was very angry. He shook his fist at Mrs Flip and shouted, "I shan't come to your party now! I just shan't come!"

"Well, don't then!" said Mrs Flip, and she went inside and banged her door. Chinky banged his.

Soon there was the sound of chimes, and along came the ice-cream man. Mrs Flip heard him and out she ran. She bought the biggest ice-cream cake he had, all pink and yellow and popped it into her freezer for the party that afternoon.

And when Chinky looked out of his window at half-past four, he saw everyone busy eating ice cream in Mrs Flip's garden, as happy as could be. Wasn't he cross!

"Why didn't I go straight home as I said I would? Why did I say I wouldn't go to the party? I talk too much, that's what's the matter with me," said poor Chinky.

But chatterboxes can't be stopped – you try stopping one, and see!